Ghosts, Lies, and Videotape

Ghosts, Lies, and Videotape

A Ravenmist Whodunit
Book Three

BY OLIVIA JAYMES

www.OliviaJaymes.com

Chapter One

SPRING IN THE Midwest is like no other place on earth. There isn't a linear progression from snow to tulips. It's more like two steps forward and one – or five – steps back. It's cold, then it's warm for a day, then it's cold again for a week, then it's warm again but this time for two days, then it's *freezing* cold, then it's warm again…

Do I need to go on? I think you get the idea.

Today was a warm and sunny day and I was so happy not to be wrapped up in layers that I was practically singing showtunes. That's pretty gosh darn happy.

Oops! I haven't introduced myself. How rude.

I'm Theodosia "Tedi" Hamilton and I own the Ravenmist Inn, a rambling old Victorian that's been in my father's family for generations. The entire property consists of several acres and six restored buildings. I'm also the president of the local paranormal society and I'll answer your question before you even have to ask it. Yes, ghosts are real.

How do I know? So glad you asked.

I have a ghost – Terrence – that lives in my closet which

means that I now dress in the bathroom. Other than that minor inconvenience it's rather interesting to have a ghost in residence.

The whole town of Ravenmist, Illinois is, in fact, crazy haunted and I've spoken to several spirits now. As I'd been warned, most ghosts are pretty much as they were in life. If they were nice when they were alive, they're nice as ghosts. If they were jerks? They aren't any better in the afterlife.

The people that walked through the front door of my inn were also representative of the population at large. Some were nice and polite, others angry and difficult. I was expecting to get both sides of the coin today as we had a rush of guests checking in. Most were here for the film festival that was happening at the local movie theater. It was a yearly event and quite popular with cinema buffs in several neighboring counties. A few were actors in the movies and with them came a whole slew of issues, one of which was standing in my lobby and causing a ruckus.

The press.

Now don't get me wrong. *The press* in Ravenmist is a guy named Gus and when he takes a vacation there's no newspaper until he returns. One extra man in my inn wasn't going to be a problem, but today I had more than that.

Today I had out of town press in my lobby. Several of them. All trying to get a famous actor's picture and a quote. There were flashbulbs and people talking loudly over one another and I was starting to get a nasty headache just watching the entire circus.

Added to all of that were the fans that had been camped out on my front steps before dawn just to get a glimpse of their heartthrob. They were also in my lobby trying to get their own photos or maybe an autograph. It was semi-controlled chaos. At the center of all of it was the famous and handsome actor Brock Mandrell, and he appeared to be loving the attention. He had a huge smile on his face as he signed pieces of paper and took selfies with the crowd all the while answering softball questions from the reporters.

Frankly, I didn't care if he did his own stunts. But he proudly answered that he did.

"Tedi, there's someone that wants to speak with you."

Annie, my front desk clerk, had tapped me on the shoulder and I gratefully turned away from the informal press conference currently taking place. It always put a bee in my bonnet when grown women acted like rabid teenagers over a man.

"Of course, what do they need?"

A short man with a thinning hairline stepped forward. "I'm Bill Warner, Brock's agent, and this is his wife Laura."

The woman was absolutely stunning with long dark hair and a perfectly made up face. She was also a tad overdressed for midafternoon in a small town. We don't normally wear sequins until after five o'clock but she certainly looked good in them.

"Nice to meet you. How can I help you?"

"I just wanted to check on the security arrangements."

"Security arrangements," I repeated, shaking their hands. "Can you be more specific?"

"What sort of arrangements do you have here for the safety of your guests?"

Oh, *those* arrangements.

"We have deadbolt locks on all the guestroom doors. There are chains, too."

Warner opened his mouth but no sound came out. The wife looked rather stunned as well.

"I–I'm not sure I understand," he finally replied, his hand fluttering to his chest. "That's it? That's all?"

"Ravenmist doesn't have much of a crime problem," I explained, completely ignoring the three murders since last October. Those were a fluke. "In fact, most people don't even lock their doors or cars."

Although I did lock my car. Not because I thought someone might steal it, but because the last time that I'd left it unlocked one of my cooks had used the backseat to take a nap between lunch and dinner. He'd scared the bejesus out of me when I climbed into the car. Turns out his was the exact same color and model.

"But...you have all of these famous people staying here..."

The man's voice trailed away and he seemed at a loss.

"I do have security cameras around the property," I replied. I'd installed them after the Valentine Ball in February. Jack, our local sheriff, had convinced me that it was a good idea. I still wasn't sure.

"It's fine, Bill. No one is going to harass Brock in this tiny little town. I don't think they even have a Starbucks," Laura laughed.

"Five blocks to the east, next to the grocery store. Now I can assure you that we've had hundreds of guests from the festival here at the Ravenmist Inn and we've never had any trouble. If anyone gets out of line, my bartender Doug will escort them off the premises. If it gets really bad, we would of course call in Sheriff Garrett."

Warner didn't appear convinced but Laura was relaxed and smiling.

"I'm sure you're right," she said with a nod. "Brock will be fine. He just loves the attention."

I could see that.

"If anyone gives you any problems at all, please just let me or one of my staff know. We don't tolerate any sort of harassment here."

This time the man did seem somewhat mollified. He pulled out his phone from his pocket and began to scroll through it. "I do seem to remember that we had the sheriff in this town checked out. A real no-nonsense type. Maybe we should go talk to him."

That was an interesting description. No nonsense. It certainly fit Jack.

"Two blocks west. Is there anything else I can do for you?"

They were anxious to go talk to Jack so I bid them a good day, made sure I pointed them in the right direction, and headed for my personal apartment that took up most of the first floor. My mom and I were attending the film festival tonight and I needed to get showered and dressed. I was excited as one of my friends from college – Sasha – had a role in one of the movies.

She was also staying at the inn but she'd gone straight to the festival from the airport, sending her luggage ahead. I'd put her in a lovely corner room with a view of the back-patio area.

I kicked off my shoes at the door and breathed a sigh of relief. I was finally alone. Sort of.

"You're going to the film festival, aren't you?"

The voice was close by but I couldn't see Terrence, my very own resident spirit. He usually hung out in my living room watching old movies on cable but today he'd been notably absent. In fact, I'd barely seen him the entire week.

"I am," I responded, pulling out the dress I planned on wearing. "With my mom. What are you planning to do tonight?"

"I'm going too."

Wait...what?

"I'VE SAVED UP all of my energy today," Terrence explained for the second time. I hadn't quite comprehended the first. He still hadn't shown himself and now I knew why. "Why shouldn't I go? I love movies and it's open to the public. I'm the public."

Yes...albeit a deceased one.

Think, think, think. Think of a decent argument to change his mind.

"What if someone finds out that you're a ghost?"

"How will they know? No one figured out Edward was a ghost on Valentine's Day. I have enough energy to look completely alive."

That was true. The supernatural energy in Ravenmist was at unheard of levels currently. The dead walked around town as if they were still alive and no one had a clue that they were interacting with ghosts. If anything, they thought they needed a little sun.

My best friend Missy and I had been trying to do some research as to what could be causing all of this energy but so far, we'd come up empty. Her grandmother had given us a contact but there had been no answer on that telephone number. We'd left a message back in February and hadn't heard a peep. At this point, we didn't expect to so we were looking for a new route to go down.

"You just want to keep me here."

That wasn't fair.

"Now wait a minute," I said with a heavy sigh. "I don't want to keep you here. I'm just worried about you, that's all. I don't want anything to happen to you."

"What terrible thing could happen to me, Tedi? I'm already dead."

Well…that was a good question.

"Probably nothing except that you all would be exposed and the whole town would know of your existence."

"Edward and I have already thought about that." His tone was reasonable and calm, not in the least belligerent. "They can't get rid of us. It's our home, too. That's why we've been working on our documentary."

Documentary? This was the first I'd heard of it.

"You're making a documentary? About what?"

"Edward found a video camera at the bookstore and we've been making a film about our lives in the in-between. It's sort of an educational movie to inform those still alive about their options when they die. Also, we want them to understand that they don't have to be afraid or anything. We're just like them."

Minus a heartbeat.

"Some people aren't going to understand, Terrence. What if they do one of those ceremonies where they scare away ghosts? I've seen those on television."

"I seriously doubt they're real. I can't think of anything that could make me leave. Maybe it would be for the best if people knew about us. No one would have to hide."

These words were surprising considering that Terrence didn't even like to leave the grounds of the inn, but he'd been coming out of his shell ever so slowly. A few weeks ago, he'd walked through the lobby of the inn and out into the backyard right in front of several guests.

"I'm not sure some people would be able to handle the truth."

He didn't say anything else and I couldn't see his expression to be able to tell if he was angry or frustrated, or perhaps he'd already left the room.

"Terrence? Are you mad?"

"No, Tedi. I understand your concerns but we're determined to make this documentary. We want to be understood."

I wasn't going to change his mind and now that I was really thinking about it, I wasn't sure that I should be trying. This was his afterlife and if he wanted to venture out to a film festival or make a movie then that's what he should be able to do.

"I hope you have a good time. And good luck with your project."

It looked like I was going to have to get used to seeing my ghost in social settings.

That's not weird at all, right?

Chapter Two

MY MOTHER PEGGY Hamilton was a huge movie buff and she was the real reason I'd attended the film festival years ago for the first time. Now we went together and it was a lovely bonding time for us. I didn't get to spend near enough time with her – or my dad who was currently in Miami visiting his new girlfriend – as we all had such busy schedules. Mom had always been quite the social butterfly but now that she and my father were getting a divorce she was hardly ever home. It's not easy to admit that your own mother had far more of a personal life than you do.

We had, however, never attended a pre-film cocktail party. They were usually reserved for people in the industry, critics, local VIPs, and such, but because of my friendship with Sasha we were smack dab in the middle of one fancy-dancy party. There was finger food, champagne, and a string quartet playing in the corner of the opulent lobby. The theater had been restored from its original art deco glory and it was almost like stepping back in time. But with cell phones.

I'd snagged champagne for both of us and we were sipping

the bubbly golden liquid as we scanned the crowd for anyone we might know.

"I'm just saying that you could do worse."

My mother had decided that this was a great time to convince me that Jack was the perfect man.

"Gee, thanks, Mom. I always know who to go to when I'm feeling a little down on myself."

"The sheriff—"

"Is just my friend. That's it. Friends. Stop matchmaking. I don't want to be matched."

Since my divorce it had been one of my mother's goals to see me hitched again. I'm not sure why. She hadn't thought much of my ex David. She said she couldn't trust a man who didn't like chocolate. Turns out she was right. Lesson learned.

As for Sheriff Jackson Garrett, I didn't think he was in a hurry to find true love either. Friendship was good enough for the two of us.

"You don't have to marry him, but wouldn't it be nice to have a man in your life? Someone to talk to? Someone to rub your shoulders when you're tired and make you tea when you're sick?"

"Men do that?"

This was big, important news.

"Some do."

"I seriously doubt Jack makes tea."

"I'm sure he has many fine qualities."

"If I agree can we change the subject to anything else but my love life?"

A passing waiter held out a silver tray and I helped myself to a small canapé with mushrooms.

"How about we talk about your love life? Are you still dating the high school principal?"

My mom was rocking sixty, and didn't look a day over fifty. I could only hope to be that good looking in thirty years or so. I asked her the secret once and she said it was sunscreen and good friends. I now make a point to have both.

"Everett? Not anymore. But your father and I are getting a divorce, Theodosia. I'm allowed to go out on dates. He's seeing someone. Why aren't you getting on his case?"

"What makes you think I don't?"

"How about we change the subject yet again," my long-suffering mother sighed. "Are you excited to see your friend's movie?"

"Absolutely, this is the biggest role she's ever had."

The movie might be indie but it had a big star as the lead in Brock Mandrell. That meant it was getting attention that other films might not. The last role I'd seen my friend in was Waitress Number Two in a huge summer blockbuster. She'd been saved by a superhero.

I took a sip of the chilled champagne, the bubbles tickling my nose and throat. Delicious. I should do this every single day, and maybe eat bonbons while I bark out orders to my staff from a brocade fainting couch.

No? Sigh. Okay, but you're shattering my dreams.

"Tedi! There you are."

Jogging down a red velvet sweeping staircase was my friend Sasha. More gorgeous than any one person should be allowed to be, she made descending a flight of stairs a theatrical event. At least it appeared that way as everyone milling about had stopped what they were doing to turn and watch her, all agog.

If I didn't adore Sasha so much, I would have to hate her guts. She was everything I'd ever wanted to be – tall, thin, with long dark hair and piercing blue eyes with a thick fringe of lashes that owed nothing to mascara. She somehow managed to look chic and put together in that incredible effortless way that probably took a heck of a lot of work behind the scenes.

She was also sweet as pie, smart as a whip, and generous to a fault. In summary, Sasha was my friend and for good reason. She pulled me into a giant hug that had me choking for air.

"Girl, ease up," I teased when she finally let me go. "You've been working out. You almost hugged the stuffing out of me. I'm a fragile flower."

"I've missed you," she sighed. "You're so down to earth and my life these days is anything but."

She'd shared a few stories over email and that was an understatement of woolly mammoth proportions. Sasha was living a life I couldn't even fathom.

"You remember my mom Peggy?"

"I do," Sasha exclaimed, giving her one of those big hugs as well. "It's so good to see you again."

My mother adored Sasha and if I didn't already know I

would have been clued in by how she beamed and hugged her back.

"It's so lovely to see you too, and thank you for inviting us," Peggy replied. "I feel so Hollywood in this beautiful old theater sipping champagne with the movie industry movers and shakers. Is there anyone famous here?"

Wrinkling her nose, Sasha nodded. "Yes, Brock is...somewhere, probably giving an interview. There's actors and directors all over the place, too. Of course, there's also lots of hangers-on that just want to be in the vicinity of the rich and famous. Be part of their entourage."

"That reminds me, your luggage showed up this morning along with all the bags from your co-stars."

Sasha grinned and clapped her hands together in glee. "I couldn't let them stay anywhere else but your wonderful inn. I told them all the haunted stories you told me years ago and about how charming the town is. I'm just sorry that I couldn't check in this morning. I came to the theatre straight from the plane. We were giving interviews until a few minutes ago."

"You get to lead the glamorous life."

"Believe me when I say that answering the same questions over and over is not in any way glamorous, but it is part of the job." She glanced over her shoulder and her face split into a grin before beckoning to someone in the crowd.

"I have to introduce you to Cara Lassiter. She's also in the movie, and she was my best friend on set." A lovely woman with long dark blonde hair and big blue eyes joined us. She looked around my own age but far more attractive. "Cara, this is Tedi and her mother Peggy. This is Cara Lassiter. You may have seen her on 'A Life Well Loved'."

Everyone had heard of "A Life Well Loved", one of the few soap operas – oops, I mean daytime drama – still on the air. My mom used to watch it every day when I was a kid and for all I knew she still did.

Peggy looked like she was going to explode. So…yep, clearly my mom knew Cara Lassiter. Her eyes were sparkling and she was practically hopping up and down in her cocktail dress and heels.

"You're Angela Baldwin," Peggy gasped, her eyes wide. "Oh my God, I love you."

Giving my mom the side eye, I held out my hand. "It's nice to meet you. Sorry about my mom. She's a big fan of the show. Has been for years."

Cara smiled and shook our hands. "It's fine. I haven't been on it in awhile. My character is in a coma."

"Are you ever going to get out of that coma?" my mother asked, her brows knitted together in concern. I hoped that I wouldn't have to remind my mother that Cara – or Angela – wasn't actually in a coma. "That nasty Steven should be in prison for running you off the road."

Laughing, Cara simply shrugged. "Who knows with these storylines? Right now, I'm happy making movies. If they asked me back, I might consider it though. It was steady work and that's hard to find in this business."

"Cara is staying at the inn, too," Sasha said, her arm around the woman's shoulder. "She's the extra that I called you about. Her luggage should be with mine."

"I got your message and she's in the room next to yours," I assured my friend. "When you get there your keys are at the front desk."

"I appreciate the accommodation," Cara said. "I was going to stay with a friend in a town nearby but that didn't work out."

"It's fine. We had a last-minute cancellation. Brock Mandrell was planning to bring his publicist but apparently he has the flu and can't make it."

Sasha rolled her eyes. "More likely, his publicist doesn't want to be around him any more than anyone else. Brock Mandrell is a real pill."

Cara nodded in agreement. "And handsy. I had to tell him that if he didn't watch it, he'd be pulling back a stump."

"Good for you," my mother said. "I hadn't heard that he was like that."

"It's a not very well-kept secret in the industry," Sasha explained. "The fact is, he's difficult to work with but he sells tickets so they put up with it. To his co-stars he's a whiny, spoiled brat, to the studio he's box office gold. In fact, there's Darrell over there with his assistant. He's the director of the picture and Brock was his problem for the ten-week shoot. I thought they were going to kill each other at one point."

Darrell Kennedy was much younger than I'd pictured a director would be. He was probably in his late twenties or early thirties, with a mop of wild brown curls on top of his head and dressed like he'd just worked a day in the fields complete with ripped, faded jeans and a red and blue plaid shirt that was buttoned wrong.

In contrast, the young woman next to him was dressed and coiffed perfectly, just as one would expect in Hollywood. She was the three Bs – blonde, blue-eyed, and buxom.

Sasha looked around the crush of bodies in the lobby. "It's weird that Brock isn't here. Normally he loves the attention and likes to work the room."

Cara glanced at her watch and then nodded toward the double doors that led to the theatre. "We should take our seats. The movie will start soon."

I rubbed my hands together and smiled. "I can't wait to see it."

"Neither can I," my mom declared. "Let's go."

We followed Sasha and Cara into the main theater and sat down about halfway from the back and front, me on the aisle, then Mom, and then Cara. Sasha was still hovering in the aisle.

"Hey, I'll join you in a few minutes," she said, her gaze going to the back of the theater. "There's someone I need to talk to for a minute. Save my seat."

"Will do."

I shoved my purse into the seat next to Cara, fidgeting on the cushion to find the comfiest spot for the next two hours.

My mom's elbow dug into my ribs. "Look, it's the sheriff."

Jerking my head to the left, I could see two familiar people walking down the middle aisle, right past me, and sitting a few rows down.

Sheriff Jackson Garrett and his teenaged son Tyler.

"We should go and say hello."

Tugging at my mother's arm, I pulled her back down into her seat. "Not now. Maybe later."

"Why–"

Luck was with me because the lights began to dim and my mother sighed and surrendered. For now. She'd be dragging me over there the minute the credits were finished.

And what was he doing here anyway? Was he following me? I didn't even know he liked movies. Or people. Or fun of any kind. He was usually against all of that in Ravenmist. Perhaps he had a doppelgänger? And Tyler liked to hang out with him?

Right. Lame theory.

What was he doing at a film festival?

Seriously…why was Jack here?

THE MOVIE BEGAN and I was pulled in by Sasha's portrayal of a woman torn in two directions. About halfway through the picture she went out to dinner with her boyfriend, the brother of Brock's character. There was a rain of gunfire on the sidewalk in front of the restaurant and she fell, her dead body sprawled on the wet pavement as the metaphorical rain came down from the gray sky. Brock's character cackled triumphantly; his expression gleeful. He then went out to dinner as if nothing happened with his naive girlfriend, played by Cara, who didn't have a clue that he was a criminal.

Sasha slipped into the seat next to mom and leaned across, whispering, "No one can find Brock. Darrell's about to blow a gasket."

"Maybe he wasn't feeling well," my mother suggested softly. "He might have stepped outside for some fresh air."

"He's playing the diva again," Sasha grumbled, turning back to watch the screen. "He's getting more attention not showing up than if he did."

The film continued and Brock's character became even worse, shooting first and not bothering to ask questions later. His brother confronted him and a shouting match ensued, until the brother pulled a gun. Brock's character only laughed, confident that his sibling wouldn't have the guts to pull the trigger.

We were all on the edge of our seats when a man stumbled down the middle aisle of the theater and stood in front of the large screen as if he was part of the scene.

"That's Brock," Sasha whispered. The rest of the crowd must also have recognized him because I could hear them become restless, a low hum of conversation despite the loud movie dialogue. "Oh my God, what is he doing?"

That was a good question. Whatever was happening in front of us, the projection room hadn't taken note of so the film continued to flicker on the screen and Brock stood there for a long moment before crumpling to the floor. A collective gasp went up and finally the theater lights went on, the movie cut off abruptly. Darrell, the director, had sprinted down to the front and was kneeling next to Brock's prone body, cajoling the actor to stand up.

"Is he drunk?" my mother asked, leaning closer to me so that no one else would hear. "Is he taking something?"

The director sat back on his heels and heaved a heavy breath, his shoulders sagging and his head hanging. He said something we couldn't hear to his assistant and then turned to the audience.

"He's been shot. Brock Mandrell is dead."

Chapter Three

THERE WAS AN ambulance and the police, of course. Jack and his well-trained deputies descended on the theater and pushed all of us into the lobby where the management plied us with free food and champagne to keep us from rebelling. The cops wanted to speak with all of us before we would be allowed to leave and not everyone was happy about that. There was a great deal of teeth gnashing and a few people throwing their industry weight around but I knew that Jack wouldn't care about Hollywood glamour.

He was going to speak to us one by one and no one was getting out of here until they did. End of story.

Most of us didn't have much to say since all we knew was that we'd been watching a movie and then Brock Mandrell had stumbled in and died. The director and actors in the film had been separated into a room upstairs and Sasha had begged Mom and I to accompany her since she didn't have any family here.

"I'm shocked that they let us in," I said as we settled onto a large overstuffed couch. According to Sasha this was the press room where they'd all given interviews earlier.

Sasha nodded toward the deputy at the door. His name was Frank and I'd gone to high school with him.

"I told him you were my sister and that your mom was my mom. I hope that's okay."

Peggy smiled and patted my friend's hand but I couldn't help but bark with laughter. Frank hadn't been the brightest bulb in the box but I would have thought he would have remembered my other sisters. "He must have mixed you up with someone else. We went to school together."

"He didn't even question it."

If Jack knew, he'd have a cow. He liked to run a tight ship.

Mom's gaze darted around the room. "Where's Cara?"

As if on cue, the door to the room opened and Cara walked in, her face tearstained and her eyes red with Jack at her side. He didn't have his usual scowl in place which was a surprise, considering there had been another murder in Ravenmist. He actually looked…nice. Almost sympathetic. He leaned down to say something to her and she nodded, dabbing a tissue to her eyes. And where was Tyler? Had Jack sent him home?

I didn't have time to ponder the question as Jack was done with Cara apparently and had moved on to Sasha.

"Miss Erskine, I'm Sheriff Jack Garrett. May I ask you a few questions?"

"Of course," Sasha agreed. "And please call me Sasha."

Jack glanced at my mother and myself. "Perhaps we should do this in private?"

In other words…he wanted us to leave. Nice try, Jack, but

no cigar.

"I'd like them to stay," Sasha said, a quiver in her voice. "Is it a problem?"

For a minute I thought he was going to say yes, but then he nodded curtly and pulled out that little notebook he liked to write in when someone was murdered.

"Sasha, I do have a few questions for you so take your time answering, okay? Now, where were you during the movie?"

"In the audience."

Jack scratched something down on the paper, the sound of his pencil loud in the quiet room.

"But you weren't there the whole time."

He sort of made it sound like a question that he already knew the answer to. Having listened to Jack question suspects, I knew where he was going. I moved a little closer to Sasha and placed my arm around her shoulder. It was only the second question and she already appeared to have a deer in the headlights expression.

"No, I went outside to make a phone call."

"And who did you call?"

"My boyfriend." Sasha reached down and fumbled in her bag that had been placed on the floor. "You can check my phone. I'm telling the truth."

"We will check, thank you. Now after the call, what did you do?"

"I went into the theater to watch the movie."

"And we can vouch for that, Detective," my mother said to

Jack, patting Sasha's hand. "She sat with us."

"That's good. The whole time?"

"The whole time," I echoed. "Until...you know."

The dead body.

"I know."

He wrote down something else that I couldn't see from this angle. "Now Sasha, did you and the deceased get along?"

I could feel her stiffen beside me. "If you're asking if we're friends, the answer is no. We were co-workers. Nothing more."

"Happy co-workers?"

I could feel my own hackles rising. Just get to it. I decided to give him a prod.

"Are you going somewhere with this, Jack, or are you just running laps?"

It probably wasn't a good idea to antagonize the sheriff of our small and close-knit community but I didn't like his line of questioning. He obviously thought that Sasha had something to hide.

"We made a movie together," she finally answered, her lips pressing together into a thin line. "Brock wasn't a friend and we didn't spend any free time together."

"Did you ever argue?"

Okay, I'd had enough.

"I don't think you should–"

"No, it's okay." Sasha shook her head, a few tears slipping down her cheeks. "Yes, he and I argued. He was a difficult person to be around at times. But if you're asking if I killed him the answer is no. I'm guessing, however, there are hundreds of boyfriends and husbands that wanted him dead. He had an eye for the ladies and he didn't care if they were already attached, if you know what I mean."

Jack's lips twisted. "I do know what you mean. Thank you. Please don't leave town in case I have any other questions. Where can I get a hold of you?"

"She's staying with me at the Ravenmist Inn."

"Fine. I'll send an officer over to check your phone, Miss Erskine. Thank you again for your time. Peggy and Tedi, I may have some questions for you later."

Oh goody. At least this time the murder didn't happen at the inn.

Jack stood and paused for a moment. "Do you happen to know where the director Darrell Kennedy is? I need to speak with him also."

Sasha scanned the room, a frown on her face. "He was here at one point. Maybe he's just outside in the hall talking a call or something?"

"You're probably right. I'll have my deputies check the building again. Thank you for your time. If I have any more questions, I'll be in touch."

Jack turned and headed straight for the director's assistant who was currently comforting Cara on the sofa in the corner.

"He thinks I'm a suspect," Sasha said, falling back against the cushions and covering her face with her hands. "This is terrible. I'll never work in Hollywood again."

"No one is going to blame you."

"Bad press is going to kill any career I might have had."

"It won't get that far. When Jack finds who did it, you'll be in the clear."

"What if they don't find the killer?"

"Then we'll find him."

I did have a little experience at that, after all.

I HAD JUST visited the ladies room of the theater and was heading back to pick up Peggy and Sasha when I spotted Jack out of the corner of my eye striding down the hallway.

"Jack," I called out, hurrying to catch up with him. "Can I talk to you for a second?"

He made a growling noise and scraped his fingers through his hair, the universal sign for frustration. "Make it fast, Tedi. I'm trying to find Darrell Kennedy."

"Fine, I will make it fast." I crossed my arms over my chest and gave him my best mean look. "Sasha did not do this so don't even go there. I've known her since college and she wouldn't even step on spiders back then. She isn't capable of killing someone. She just isn't. Look somewhere else. Brock Mandrell wasn't all that popular. There must be several suspects."

Quirking an eyebrow at my outburst, Jack appeared amused. "Are you telling me my job now, Tedi? Really? Are you sure you want to do that?"

Straightening my spine so I looked as tall as possible, I met his stare and didn't flinch. "I think that I do. I could tell from your questions that you have Sasha on your suspect list."

"And you're telling me to take her off?"

He was definitely laughing at me.

"You'd be wasting your time and I know how much you hate that."

Nodding slowly, he chuckled. "Yes, I do. I'll take your advice into consideration. Now are we done here? Because I have a killer to catch."

It wasn't any fun when I couldn't get him at least a little mad.

"I guess so. Who are you going to speak to next?"

"We're not going to do this."

"Do what?"

"This."

"This what?"

Jack blew out a slow breath. "We are not going to talk about my investigation, Tedi. You are not a part of it. Stay out of it, and this time I mean it. Don't stick your nose where it doesn't belong. This could be dangerous."

"Of course, I'm not a part of it," I protested. "I just want to make sure that Sasha is treated fairly."

For a split second I thought I saw a flash of hurt in Jack's eyes but it was gone so quickly I must have imagined it. "You think I treat people unfairly?"

"No. No, not at all." Darn it, I had hurt his feelings. I didn't mean to but I could see how he would take offense. "I'm just really worried about my friend."

"If she's done nothing wrong, she doesn't have anything to worry about. Just counsel her to tell the truth and she'll be fine."

"I will." We both stood there staring at each other, neither one of us saying anything until I broke the silence. "What were you and Tyler doing here anyway? I didn't know you liked film festivals."

Jack shrugged. "Tyler is interested in being a filmmaker. A director, I guess. It's better than last year when all he wanted to be was a YouTube star. He's interviewing a few people at the festival for a school paper, and I'm trying to be a supportive parent."

"You looked pretty supportive to me."

"I'm trying. Now I really do have to go, but do me a favor."

I really wanted to make up for hurting his feelings.

"Of course. Name it."

"If you see the director, give me a call. I'm assuming he's staying at the inn and we haven't been able to find him anywhere."

"He is and I will. Anything else I can do?"

He leaned down until we were almost nose to nose. "No, because you're not a part of the investigation. Stay out of it, Tedi."

Easier said than done. I wouldn't let a murder ruin my friend's career. If Jack couldn't find the guilty party, then I would.

Chapter Four

JACK WAS ONCE again sucking up free food in my kitchen when I found him a few hours later. I'd been looking for him everywhere including the sheriff's station but I should have known that he'd be here. Murder always made him ravenous.

"I found him."

My announcement didn't make the sheriff jump with excitement. If anything, he picked up a french fry and bit into it with relish. "What did you find?"

"Him. Darrell Kennedy. Didn't you want to talk to him?"

Finally. I had his attention. The fries were forgotten which was a relief. I was worried about Jack's cholesterol. He had the palate of a teenage boy and was constantly eating way too much fried food. He would drop dead before he was fifty. And he'd probably do it at the inn just to spite me. Then he'd haunt me forever because he was far too stubborn to cross into the light.

Quickly wiping his mouth with a paper napkin, he pushed his half-empty plate away. "I do want to talk to him. Where is he?"

"His room. He's holed up there and won't come out. One of

the maids tried to drop off more towels and he's deadbolted the door."

Muttering under his breath, Jack breezed by me with barely a glance. His heavy footsteps echoed on the refinished hardwood floors that were older than both of us. Combined.

"Slow down," I called after him, jogging to catch up. "He won't come out. I've already tried."

He didn't even pause. "That's the difference between you and me, Tedi. You asked nicely. I'm not planning to."

"Do you have a warrant?"

I sounded out of breath because keeping up with him had winded me. I really needed to think about exercising. Something besides jumping to conclusions.

This time he did stop, and I almost ran into his back. "What would I need a warrant for? I just want to talk to him."

"I don't think he wants to talk to you, Jack."

"I'm not really focused on what he wants right now. Not when I have a murder to solve."

"You can't drag him out of there."

"You're right." We'd reached the top of the stairs and Jack paused, waiting for me to tell him where to go.

"End of the hall. Last door on the left."

In my absence a few guests had gathered outside of the door. Laura Mandrell, wife to Brock. Brock's agent. Darrell's assistant. And Cara. They all appeared to be pleading with the director to come out and talk to the sheriff.

"Excuse me, folks." Jack stepped between them and they

parted like the Red Sea. "I'd like to speak to Mr. Kennedy."

Laura Mandrell shook her head, her cheeks red. "He won't come out."

Jack stepped right next to the door and spoke in a booming voice. "Are you sure he won't come out?"

I swear the building shook he was so loud. My ears would be ringing for hours.

"Someone should tell Mr. Kennedy that not talking to me makes him look guilty. If he's innocent and doesn't have anything to hide, he shouldn't have a problem answering a few questions. But it's up to him, of course. If the press asks me, I'll just have to tell them that he refused to speak to me."

Ah, I see what you did there.

Then that crazy like a fox sheriff sauntered away from the door and back down the hallway toward me. It only took a moment for the door to fly open and Darrell Kennedy to pop out, a scared and frantic expression on his face and his curly hair standing on end.

"Wait. You can't tell them that. I'll be finished."

Jack allowed a small smile to turn up the corners of his lips and then he gave me a wink before turning back to the panicked director.

"Mr. Kennedy? I'm Sheriff Jack Garrett. I have a few questions for you, if you don't mind. Tedi, can we use the sitting room?"

Yes, you can, Sheriff. By all means.

JACK LIKED TO use my sitting room to question his suspects and it was fine by me. The Ravenmist Inn had been through multiple renovations and at one point an addition had been built onto the main building. An external window was now in my walk-in closet and my Gran had simply hung a curtain over it in the sitting room instead of boarding it over. Little did she know that I would be using it to listen in to Jack's interrogations.

Pushing aside a pair of leather boots, I pressed closer to the wall so I didn't have to strain to hear. So far Jack had asked a few warm-up questions that Darrell was easily able to answer.

"Where were you during the movie, Mr. Kennedy?"

"Just call me Darrell. Everybody does."

"Okay, Darrell. Where were you doing the movie?"

"I was watching it. In the theater."

"The whole time?"

A small pause.

"Not the whole time."

"Can you expand on that?"

From the even longer pause I kind of had the feeling Darrell Kennedy didn't want to.

"I was watching the movie and then I got a text from Brock to meet him outside near the front doors. I'd been looking for him because he wasn't around before the movie to talk to this interviewer from a major magazine."

"How far into the movie were you?"

"I'm not sure."

What a lame answer. Jack, don't accept a stupid answer like that. He's hiding something.

"Darrell, you're the director of the film, are you not?"

"I am."

"Then how could you be unsure as to how far into the movie you were? You made the movie."

"It's just that...I wasn't really paying attention. I was texting with my wife in San Francisco. I've already seen the film several times so there was no reason to watch..."

"You didn't even glance up at the screen?"

"Not really."

"You said that you were on your phone, correct? Texting?"

"Yes."

"The time is displayed on the phone screen, Darrell. What time was it?"

Haha. Got him. Jack was pretty decent at this.

"I–Well–I think it was around eight o'clock but I'm not sure."

Kennedy didn't seem sure of a lot of things.

"Okay, let's say it was around eight. So you got a text from our victim. What did you do?"

"I got up and went outside to meet him."

"And was he waiting for you?"

"No, he wasn't. I stood there for a few minutes and then sent him a text wondering where he was. He didn't answer so I made a phone call. That's when... I guess that's when Brock died."

"Was there anyone else that saw you?"

"Outside?"

Kennedy sounded scandalized at the thought.

"Yes, can anyone vouch for your whereabouts when Brock Mandrell was shot and killed?"

Another silence.

"No. I was alone. But I couldn't have shot Brock," he protested, indignation in his tone. "I've never shot a gun before. Ever. And if I'd shot him in the lobby or even upstairs don't you think someone would have heard?"

"With the movie as loud as it was, I'm not certain that's the case. Now let me ask you one more question. Is it true that you and Brock argued earlier today during the press interviews?"

"It was a small disagreement. I wouldn't characterize it as an argument."

"What were you arguing about?"

"Listen, Brock has…I mean, had…a big ego. Sometimes he could be difficult to work with or even be around. Actors can be like that but I'm used to it."

"So if I ask around the cast, they'll say that you and Brock got along fine."

"Sure. Yeah. We weren't friends or anything…"

"But you never argued?"

There was a loud sigh before Kennedy answered. "Listen, I'm gonna tell you the honest truth, although I hate to speak ill of the dead. Brock Mandrell was a jerk. A real pain in the rear. Everyone thought so. So if you're looking for suspects based on who didn't like him, you're going to be really busy. Try asking his wife Laura about the divorce she was planning. You could ask his agent how Brock humiliated him in a room full of studio executives. Or Sasha and Cara about having to slap his hands away every five minutes. You could even ask my assistant how he made her life a misery every day on the set with his petty and outrageous demands. No one liked him. He once had a dog and even he tried to run away. They ended up giving the canine to Brock's brother and his kids."

Brock Mandrell sounded like a charmer. A real people person.

"So you admit you had a reason to be angry with him?"

"Everyone had a reason to be angry with him. I can't think of one person who liked him. But...that doesn't mean that I killed him. I'm a pacifist, man. I meditate. I hate guns. I abhor violence. I'm a peace-loving guy."

"Who makes incredibly violent movies."

"That's what sells. Are we done?"

"Yes, but I may have more questions. Don't leave town."

"I'm here for the festival. I'm not going anywhere. Brock's death just made my movie a box office smash."

Ouch. The cynicism was painful. Brock Mandrell might have been a loathsome human being but Darrell Kennedy was no citizen of the year, either.

There was no way that Jack could still think Sasha was a murderer after talking to this director. And what about all those other people that Darrell named? I needed to take a closer look at them. I'd start with the wife.

Chapter Five

I HAD THE best of intentions to seek out Laura Mandrell and talk to her but my best friend Missy – owner of the local bookstore – was waiting for me downstairs. The minute I saw her standing in the middle of my office talking to Howard the Fern I could have slapped myself. As the Grim Reaper in five counties, she would have escorted Brock's soul to the light. He might have seen his killer and hopefully she remembered to ask him before he crossed over…whichever way he was going.

She started talking as soon as I closed the door behind me. "I got the call."

The call was code for a dead body. She would receive a text and then somehow "appear" where she needed to be. Being the local Grim Reaper was a family business, according to Missy. Her uncle in Sarasota was the actual Grim Reaper, but a little like Santa Claus he had helpers everywhere. Sometimes a soul didn't want to cross over. They became ghosts and we had plenty of them in Ravenmist. I assumed that there were spirits all across the globe.

"I don't suppose he said who killed him before he went?"

That would be too easy but I was due for some good luck.

Hands on hips, Missy gave a frustrated groan. "I have no idea. I can't get to him. He hasn't been alone for two minutes since I got the call."

"What do you mean he hasn't been alone?"

"He's surrounded by people constantly. The coroner, his wife, his agent, the press, even a few fans."

"What are the consequences of this? Is his spirit running around loose? Do we have to find him?"

New ghosts didn't have as much energy as older ones so it wasn't as easy to see them. This could prove difficult.

To my relief, Missy shook her head. "His spirit can't separate from his body until I get there."

"So what will you do?"

"I'm going to try and get him alone in the morgue. If I don't help him cross over soon, he'll be shipped back to Hollywood and he'll be in another reaper's jurisdiction. It won't reflect well on my semi-annual review."

I made my decision instantly. "How can I help?"

Dubious. That's the expression my best friend wore when I made the offer but she was also desperate, and that's probably what made her sigh and answer my question.

"I guess you could go with me. Keep an eye out for people or maybe distract them."

"I'll get my purse. I need to talk to Brock anyway. He might have seen his killer."

The drive to the small local hospital didn't take long. Missy could have just "appeared" there using her Grim Reaper supernatural powers but since I was along, we took boring old mortal transportation. We slipped in a side door and found a bank of elevators, pressing the down button. The morgue was in the basement.

Naturally.

"What's our plan?" I asked as the door slid open silently. The hallway was deserted which was a good sign.

"I don't have one. When he's alone I'll be able to feel it and I'll transform."

"What about me?"

"You can keep an eye out. If someone—"

Missy never finished her sentence, disappearing with a pop and a rush of cold air. It looked like Brock Mandrell was alone and this was her chance. Should I try to follow her? There was a large set of double doors on my left but they looked to be secured by a card reader. Since I didn't have any super cool powers I was stuck out in the hallway.

The doors of the elevator slid open and a man in scrubs stepped out carrying a clipboard. He didn't look familiar but that didn't matter. I had my marching orders.

Be a lookout. Distract until Missy was done.

The man – a doctor perhaps – was headed straight for those double doors. I couldn't let him get past me.

"Um, hey. Are you in charge here?"

Wow, I'm so smooth sometimes. I amaze myself.

He halted, a pinched look on his face as he pushed up his

heavy glasses. "I'm Dr. Bravvers. What can I do for you?"

He was brusque and not happy about being interrupted but if he was heading into the morgue…well…his patients weren't going anywhere.

Think fast. Think fast. Think fast.

"I'm Tedi Hamilton, president of the Ravenmist Paranormal Society. I was hoping to talk to you or any of your staff about any paranormal activity you might have experienced not only here at the hospital, but anywhere in town."

Dr. Bravvers' brows shot up but then a smile spread across his face. "Have you been talking to Dr. Kerry?"

Have I? Why yes, I have.

"How did you know?" I gave him my best *trust me* grin. "I was told you were the man to speak to."

"I have so many stories. I don't even know where to begin."

"And I want to hear them all. How about I buy you a cup of coffee?"

Glancing at the closed double doors, the doctor was conflicted. "I'm on duty…"

Just how long did it take to usher a soul into the light? Missy was taking forever. Was Mandrell refusing to go? All we needed was another spirit wandering around town.

"I'm so anxious to hear your stories. Have you seen a full body apparition? Heard noises? Felt cold drafts where there shouldn't be?"

"I hear noises all of the time," Dr. Bravvers said, shaking his head. "It's spooky. And cold drafts? Constantly."

"Those are the two main signs of a haunting."

The elevator doors once again slid open and Missy stood in the car, holding the door open. No Grim Reaper robes. Just her regular jeans and sweater. She was smiling so she must have had success. "Tedi, are you coming?"

"Oops, I have to go, Dr. Bravvers." I whipped a card out of my purse. I had a stash for these sorts of opportunities. "Call or email me and we can set some time up. I'd love to do an investigation."

Because if anyplace was haunted it was the freakin' morgue. The location had to be high on the creep-factor meter.

The man nodded and tucked my card into the pocket of his scrubs. "I will, thank you."

Hopping into the elevator I waved at the doctor as the doors closed. Missy and I were once again alone.

"So? How did it go?"

"He's crossed over."

"Should I ask which way?"

The stories about him from those who knew him weren't exactly complimentary...

"It's not professional for me to talk about it."

"Did you ask him who killed him?"

She shook her head. "I didn't have time. When I got there and made sure we were alone, his soul rose from his body and the light shone down. He jumped up and ran into it. There was no time to ask him anything or to explain what was happening. That's the easiest crossover I've had in months. He didn't even ask if he was dead. He just ran into the light."

Well…it was a *spotlight*.

"Where to now?" she asked as we exited the elevator.

"We need to find out the latest on the investigation."

"The Grateful Raven it is. I could use a piece of pie."

With ice cream. Next stop…the diner. The best place to get information on anything or anyone in our little hamlet.

MISSY ORDERED APPLE but I was in the mood for peach. Daisy, the proprietor of the local diner The Grateful Raven, brought out our pie herself and then sat down with us to give us the skinny about the investigation so far. The sheriff's station was only two doors down and that meant that her eatery was a haven for Jack's employees. They liked to talk while she served them their meals. Did Jack know? We assumed he did but I'd never specifically asked.

"So what do you know?" I asked, shoveling a huge bite of pie into my mouth. I was ravenous, having missed dinner. Those little finger sandwiches at the cocktail party seemed like a long time ago.

I was also yawning. I'd been up before dawn to clear away my monthly supply ordering and now all I wanted was a comfortable bed and some restful sleep.

Daisy, dressed in her usual rainbow of colors, glanced around the diner and then leaned forward so that only we could hear.

"Not a lot, actually. The sheriff told Tamera not to talk to anyone about the case, so when she came here to pick up some coffee, she said I needed to keep it a secret. I'm only going to tell you two."

"What did she say?"

"Apparently the wife doesn't have a good alibi for the time of the murder. She said she was outside making a phone call but no one can verify that yet. Also, his agent said that the couple was having marital problems and they'd separated more than once. Apparently, Laura Mandrell had spoken to a divorce attorney."

"That would make her the number one suspect," I stated. "Spouses are always the first people the cops look at."

"The sheriff spoke to the wife and she claims that she and Brock were giving their relationship a second chance, and that after the film festival they were headed to Bora Bora for a sort of second honeymoon. She said she loved her husband and would never want to kill him. She also said that she doesn't even know how to shoot a gun, and that she doesn't own one."

Bora Bora? I wasn't even sure where that was. But good for them if they were giving it another try. That was a big *if* though…

"And that agent," Daisy went on, casting another furtive glance around the half-empty diner. "When the sheriff talked to him, he admitted that Brock Mandrell was a jerk. He treated everyone around him badly but he expected them to be okay with it because he paid them well."

"Did he talk to anyone else?" Missy asked, pushing her empty plate away. "There have to be more suspects than just the wife and agent."

"And we know that he was questioning Sasha," I added. "And he talked to the director when he was at the inn."

"The sheriff talked to the director's assistant," Daisy said. "Her name is Jessica Hornsby. She's been working with Darrell Kennedy for about two years. She said that Brock and the director hated each other's guts. By the time they finished the movie, they could barely be in the same room together."

I counted off on my fingers. "So that makes three major suspects. Brock's wife, his agent, and his director. They had much stronger motives than Sasha."

My mind was still noodling on Cara and how she fit into all of this. She'd admitted that Mandrell was "handsy" and while behavior like that would make me angry, I wouldn't kill a person over it. Plus, she'd been sitting next to my mother for the entire movie. It seemed she was in the clear.

Missy elbowed me in the ribs.

"Ouch! What was that for?"

She nodded toward the door where Jack was currently entering, still wearing the grim expression from earlier, only now he had dark circles under his eyes to go with it.

"Hi Daisy, is my takeout order ready?"

"It should be, Sheriff. I'll go check and get it bagged up for you."

Daisy stood and disappeared back into the kitchen which left Jack, Missy, and me.

Missy cleared her throat and slid out of the booth. "I think I need to visit the ladies' room. Excuse me, please."

Okay, now it was just Jack and me. And tension. Lots of tension. He narrowed his eyes and shook his head.

"You should have just come ask me, Tedi."

"Ask you what?"

"The latest gossip. That's why you're here, isn't it? You should have just asked me."

Really? Had he ever talked to himself? Difficult was his middle name.

"You would have said no."

Although plying him with delicious food might have worked. It had before.

"I would have told you what I could. Some things aren't for public consumption. Just so you know, even my assistant Tamera doesn't know everything that goes on."

"So you have secrets."

"We all have secrets. Some are just bigger than others."

"Sasha didn't do it."

I couldn't help myself. I had to say it.

"Then she doesn't need to be worried. I'm in the early stages of the investigation. I haven't ruled anyone out yet, but you probably already knew that."

Daisy came back from the kitchen with a brown bag of delicious smelling food making my stomach growl and once again reminding me that I hadn't eaten dinner. This piece of pie had barely made a dent in my appetite.

"Here you go, Sheriff. I'll put it on your tab."

"Thanks, Daisy. I need to get back to work."

Without another word, Jack exited the diner. Daisy whistled and shook her head.

"He had quite the head of steam going. Did you upset him?"

"Probably," I admitted. "I told him Sasha couldn't have done it."

"That's a man that doesn't like to be told anything. You might want to give him a wide berth for a day or two."

That's exactly what I planned. I had my own investigation to do.

Chapter Six

THERE WAS A mob of reporters outside the inn when I arrived back home. What they were waiting for I had no idea. The big news had already happened, but I supposed they wanted to talk to Mandrell's wife or maybe his agent. Pulling into my reserved space, I avoided the front doors and went around to the back door near the gazebo. I didn't want to deal with the press, frankly.

Just as I was about to round the corner, I heard voices nearby. Two people...no, three were standing on the back patio. One of them was smoking a cigarette.

Dang-nabbit. I had signs that made it clear that there was no smoking allowed that close to the inn. Some people were born rebels, and others assumed that rules didn't apply to them. I took a step forward intending to march right up to them and give them a lecture, but then hesitated as their identities became clearer.

Laura Mandrell. The agent Bill Warner – he was the one smoking. The director's assistant Jessica Hornsby. What an interesting trio out for some night air.

"No one knows what's going on," Jessica was saying. "It's all fine."

"I just don't want any mistakes. It could blow everything out of the water and this is important," Laura said. "We have to be sure."

Warner, the agent tossed his cigarette butt on the patio and ground it out with his shoe. This was why I didn't allow smoking near the building. Litter. "You two worry too much. It's all under control. They don't know a thing. Now let's get inside before the press realize you're not tucked up in bed. They probably have a long-range lens on the place and we can be seen."

The trio went back inside and I took a deep breath, sagging against the side of the inn and wishing I'd shown up about five minutes earlier so I could hear the beginning of their conversation. As it was, all I'd heard was a few cryptic statements that everything was under control.

What was under control?

What kind of mistakes?

What did no one know about?

Had these three somehow conspired to kill Brock Mandrell? And if so, what was Jessica Hornsby's motive? I could understand the wife and the agent but not hers.

Secrets and more secrets. Jack had been right. Everyone had them and some were bigger than others.

Exhausted, my head wanted to go straight to bed but my feet weren't listening, instead going upstairs to Sasha's room. There was a good chance she was still awake as she was a well-known night owl, never hitting the hay until after midnight most of the time. I really needed to talk to her, tell her all I'd found out today and get her take on all of it. She was still a suspect as far as I knew. I'd just knock on her door softly. If she didn't answer, I'd wait until tomorrow.

At the top of the stairs I turned right but stopped abruptly, jumping behind a large ficus that housekeeping took care of so I wouldn't kill it. I rubbed at my eyes but the sight in front of me didn't of away.

Darrell Kennedy going into Sasha's room. At eleven forty-five at night. What was that about?

I had a few questions for my old friend and I intended to ask them first thing in the morning.

THE HEADLINES IN the morning papers and tabloids were lurid and dramatic. I couldn't turn around in the dining room without seeing a guest reading the news. It had all blown up overnight and while I still was suspicious of what Laura Mandrell might be up to, I couldn't help but feel sorry for her.

The press had been particularly vicious to the beautiful widow, all but calling her the murderer. It seemed that she and Brock had a prenuptial agreement and if she divorced him, she'd get nothing. If he died, however, she'd inherit it all. The story also detailed many of Brock's affairs, actually naming names of actresses young and old who had fallen under his spell. Honestly, I was a little nauseated reading it. Celebrity journalism wasn't what I'd call good entertainment, but it was important research for this investigation.

It was almost enough to distract me from everything that had happened yesterday and last night. Sasha, the director, Cara, Jack, and of course, Brock Mandrell.

Almost, but not quite.

"Tedi, won't you join me for breakfast?"

Cara was smiling and waving at me from a small corner table. Of course, I'd eat breakfast with her. She was Sasha's friend and that meant she was mine as well. I probably had misunderstood what I'd seen when she was talking to Jack, her hand on his arm.

"I'd love to." I sat down and one of the waitstaff immediately slapped a cup of coffee in front of me. They knew me so well. "Did you sleep okay? Is there anything you need?"

Cara wrinkled her nose. "I slept so-so. Not because of the bed or anything, the mattress was comfy and the pillows were great. It was just...you know what I mean. Everything that happened yesterday. I'm still in shock, I guess. I can't believe that Brock is dead. It's so...surreal."

"I can't argue that. I saw him die and it's still seems weird." I glanced around the dining room. "The press was pretty harsh with his widow."

Rolling her eyes, Cara took a sip of her coffee. "I half feel sorry for her and half don't. Brock had to be a nightmare to be married to, but from what I've heard she knew what she was getting into. She married him to give her career a leg up but then after they were married, he insisted that she not work and follow him around instead. But you're right, they were pretty nasty to her in the paper this morning, although I don't think anyone was shocked that they had a prenup. Brock had money before he met her so I can't imagine that he would marry without one."

The waitress came and took our order. Cara ordered an egg white omelet and a yogurt with fruit. Since I'd missed dinner last night, I ordered a stack of pancakes, a side of ham, and a croissant. With jelly. Because that was kind of a fruit. And healthy. If you squinted and didn't look too closely.

What can I say? I'll never be a skinny actress like Sasha or Cara. I like my carbs too much. Plus, this meal was really *two* meals. Dinner last night and breakfast this morning. That was my rationale for the extra calories.

Oh wait. What about the peach pie? I'd forgotten about that and everyone knows that forgotten calories don't count. It's common knowledge. It's the same for food eaten over the sink or in front of an open refrigerator. You're welcome.

We chatted about the weather and Ravenmist's ghost stories for awhile and then the waitress brought our food. I dug in as if I hadn't eaten in weeks. Cara didn't say anything about it out loud but I could feel her gaze on me when I shoveled pancakes into my mouth.

"I missed dinner last night," I finally explained when the pancakes were gone and I'd demolished the side of ham. I was currently buttering the croissant and determined to find an unused corner of my stomach to put it. "I was really hungry."

She smiled and chuckled, nodding in understanding. "I totally get that. I actually grabbed a late dinner right here in your dining room."

There was no cool or smooth way to bring up the subject that had been bugging me. We could make small talk all day long but I really wanted to know...

"I saw you talking to our sheriff Jack Garrett. You seemed like you knew him."

Shaking her head, Cara signaled for more coffee. "I just met him yesterday but he's such a nice man. So helpful and kind."

Huh? Helpful? Kind?

"You're talking about Sheriff *Jack* Garrett?"

"You're so lucky to have him. He told me he was a detective in Chicago before he came here."

He'd told Cara quite a bit already. Interesting.

"That's my understanding."

"He told me a few of the stories from that job. The one where he was shot was almost too strange to be believed."

"I know, right?"

I'd never heard that story. I'd never heard any story. In fact, getting Jack to talk about his days as a cop in Chicago had been impossible. I didn't like to admit it but I was miffed. I'd thought Jack and I were becoming friends, but he'd told Cara more about himself in one day than he'd told me in months. They'd certainly become chummy in a short time.

Checking her watch, the actress groaned. "I'm supposed to have a conference call with my agent in ten minutes so I need to get back to my room. It was so nice to have company for breakfast, Tedi. Sorry I have to run."

"No problem. I need to get some work done as well." Another question occurred to me. "Are you going to be staying through the end of the festival? With everything that's happened..."

Did I have to spell it out? Cara had an ironclad alibi. Me. And Mom. She wasn't a suspect so Jack couldn't make her stay in town.

"Actually, I wanted to talk to you about that. I was planning to leave tomorrow morning but I was thinking that I would stay until Sasha leaves. Is that okay?"

"It's fine. I'll make the change in the computer. We're glad to have you stay."

Cara clasped her hands together. "I really want to see some ghosts."

She didn't know it, but I was betting she already had. Several of them.

Stopping for a coffee refill, I headed for my office but my phone chirped in my pocket. I checked the display and saw that it was Missy.

"Hey, what's going on?"

"I'll be pulling up in front of the inn in two minutes. Meet me out front."

"I'll repeat my question. What's going on?"

I didn't really care exactly what it was, though. I had paperwork that needed to be done and I would take any excuse to ignore it for a little longer.

"Remember that medium that Gran told us about? She finally returned my call. She wants to see us right away."

We'd officially given up hope. Now we had a chance, albeit a slim one.

Maybe this woman could tell us why Ravenmist was chock full of supernatural power. We needed answers. If the good citizens ever found out that they were socializing with ghosts...

Let's just hope that secret stayed locked away.

Chapter Seven

WHEN I'D PICTURED the home of psychic medium Madame Harriet I'd had images of gothic towers, wrought iron gates, and dark clouds gathered over a gray edifice. What I saw wasn't even close.

Madame Harriet lived out in the country on a deserted two-lane road. Her long winding drive way led to a white Victorian with the loveliest wraparound porch I'd ever seen with two rocking chairs, a wicker sofa, and three lazy cats lounging on the railing. The property was lush with shade trees and in one corner of the yard there was a multi-colored swing-set that made me want to relive my childhood, recreating sunny afternoons with nothing better to do than swing and slide until my mother said it was dinnertime.

"This is charming," Missy exclaimed as we climb out of the car. "So lovely."

It really was. The lawn was impeccably maintained with shrubbery and blooming flowers. If a visitor looked closely, they might also find a few chubby garden gnomes tucked here and there. There was even a garden statue of a rabbit reading a book.

"It's adorable," I agreed, taking in the vine-covered arbor. "Not what I pictured."

"You thought it would dark and foreboding."

The voice came out of nowhere. I swear it did. One second, we were alone and the next there was a woman around my age standing on the porch. I didn't hear the door. Or footsteps. Or anything. What on earth?

"Uh...where did you come from?"

"The usual place. Now you must be Tedi and Missy. It's such a nice day I thought we'd sit outside. Is that okay? I'll bring out some tea and we can chat."

Without another word the woman turned on her heel and disappeared into the house. This time I could hear her footfalls, though. Missy and I climbed the steps and sat down on the wicker sofa. Missy spoke first.

"I think she might be more than a psychic medium."

"You think? I didn't hear her, did you?"

"Nope." Missy's eyes narrowed and she pointed to the flower garden near the arbor. "Do you see what I see?"

I hadn't been paying attention, my mind still trying to figure out the mystery that was our hostess, but now my gaze was firmly where Missy was pointing.

Those gnomes? They were *moving. Weeding the flowerbed.* And that rabbit? He was *turning the pages* of his book.

"I see it, but I'm not sure I believe it. What is this woman? Is she some sort of witch?"

"I'm not a witch."

That voice. Our hostess had done it again. Suddenly she was standing there with a tray of tea and cookies wearing an amused, almost indulgent smile. As if Missy and I were not very bright.

That might be true about me but my best friend was exceptionally smart. So I was rather aggressive when I asked my first question.

"The gnomes are moving? And the rabbit?"

Harriet set the tray down on a low table in front of us and settled into a beautifully finished maple rocking chair. "Of course, they move. Why wouldn't they?"

"Because...they're statues?" Missy said, her brows raised.

"They're as real as you and I."

I knew that I was real but I wasn't too sure about Madame Harriet.

Clearing my throat, I went in for another question. Sadly, it didn't have anything to do with why we were here.

"If you're not a witch, what are you?"

Harriet poured the tea, her brows scrunched into a frown. "Well...that's not easy to explain. I'm not a witch. Witches are a very specific entity of which I am not. I am...magical. Some mortals might refer to me as a nymph but that's simplifying the answer a bit. I have powers, some of which I am not even yet aware of. I'll come into them later in life. Suffice it to say that I am tuned into the earth and all that rests upon it. By the way, I didn't introduce myself. I'm Harriet Leeves, or as my clients call me, Madame Harriet."

"A nymph." I tried the word on for size. "Like a water

nymph?"

She shook her head and then picked up the plate of cookies, holding it out in offering. "I shouldn't even have mentioned nymphs because that's not really what I am. I only used them as a comparison because they are in tune with the earth also."

"And you're psychic? And can talk to the dead?"

She nodded. "Yes, and yes. I can hear the future that can be and I can talk directly to our past."

Madame Harriet spoke in riddles like a bad B-movie.

"I'm not sure I understand the difference."

"I can speak directly with people from the past but since the future isn't yet defined, I can only hear their voices and catch glimpses of images. Any event in the present can change the future."

"So if I walked out right now, the future would be changed?"

"No, if you stayed it would be changed."

I give up.

Talking to Harriet was like talking to one of those automated fortune telling machines at the county fair. I cast Missy a desperate look, not knowing what to say next. The psychic-medium-nymph or whatever she was appeared to be completely normal. I wouldn't have been able to pick her out of a gaggle of soccer moms at the park. She was even dressed for the part in blue jeans, a light cotton sweater, and brown loafers.

But she couldn't seem to give a straight answer to a direct question.

So Missy gave it a try.

"Harriet, my grandmother said you might be able to help us understand what's going on in Ravenmist. There's been a huge surge of supernatural energy in the last several months. The ghosts that don't cross over have so much energy they're almost solid. They can interact, talk, dance, you name it, as if they're still alive. I don't think I have to tell you that consequences could be dire if the general population found out that they could continue living their lives even after they were dead."

Harriet sipped her tea. "That's the least of your problems. You should drink the tea before it gets cold. It's very good. My cousin sends it to me from London."

The least of our problems? I didn't like the sound of that.

"We have other worries?" I asked. "What else?"

She set her cup and saucer on the table and then leaned forward, her elbows on her knees.

"First, you're absolutely right, Missy. If people were to find out that not crossing over was a viable option, there would be huge consequences. The tedium and boredom of a ghost's existence is one of the major reasons so many do eventually go into the light even when they were reluctant to do so in the beginning. Of course, many people would eagerly cross over no matter what, but it would still be chaos. No, this is a secret that must be kept."

Missy and I couldn't agree more.

"Second," she went on. "Your other problem. Since I am tuned into the earth, I felt this surge of energy and have been tracking it. I reached out to some of my...family, shall we say…and they are all in agreement. Ravenmist has been invaded by a foreign entity. You have a catalyst deeply embedded in your small community."

Missy sucked in a horrified breath. "Invaded? Like a bug?"

Harriet shook her head. "No, my dear. Like a demon."

A demon.

Now that's not something you hear every day.

WHEN A DEMON relocates to your hometown, you're bound to have a few questions, and boy, did I.

"So a demon has moved to Ravenmist?"

"Yes."

"Do they want to destroy us? Kill us? What is the goal here?"

Harriet shrugged. "Not all demons are evil, Tedi. Some are quite benevolent and live fairly quiet and normal lives. For a demon, that is. What I said was that you had a *catalyst* in your town. A catalyst can bring good, bad, or a bit of both. So far, this catalyst has brought a significant amount of paranormal energy with them, but I can't tell if it's good or evil."

"But it could be evil?"

"Yes."

"What are the odds that it is?"

"Fifty-fifty? Normally I would say seventy-thirty but so far nothing has really happened except the energy burst."

Missy and I exchanged a quick glance. Her eyes were round

with shock and horror. We had a *demon* in Ravenmist.

"Is that how demons are tracked? Energy bursts?"

Harriet refilled her tea. "Normally, demons aren't tracked at all. Honestly, the only reason I could feel the energy burst is because your town is rather rural. If that demon had stepped in New York City there would barely be a blip, although I must say that this demon is particularly powerful if they can keep up this level of energy all of the time."

"So how do we get rid of it?" Missy asked. "Is there some sort of spell or ritual? Do we have to sacrifice a chicken or something? Because I can pick up a bucket and some mashed potatoes on my way home."

Harriet scowled at Missy's query. "That's voodoo. Sacrificing a chicken won't do anything. As for getting rid of your demon, good luck. First, you'd have to identify the demon which will be impossible, but then supposing you could, you'd then have to convince them to move out of your town. One would assume they moved there because they wanted to, so I doubt you could get them to leave."

My head hurt. Straight up pounding headache right in my temples.

"So let me understand this..." I began, rubbing at my forehead with my fingertips. "We can't identify the demon because he or she looks just like us? So you're saying that demons walk among us?"

"They do. There's not many of them, thank goodness, but they talk and walk and look just like everyone else."

Missy was shaking her head. "There has to be some way of identifying them. Some mark or sign? Can they not swim? Or maybe they can't sing or something?"

"Lots of people can't sing," I reminded my friend. Myself, for example.

Harriet frowned and rubbed her chin. "There is one distinguishing feature I'm told, but it's only legend. I don't know if it's true. I heard a story that if milk is poured on their skin it will burn and smoke."

"That's…weird."

"It is a demon, dear. They're not exactly human."

"So let's say that we find this demon. How can we figure out if they're good or evil?"

"You could ask them."

Missy shook her head. "It doesn't really matter. Even if they're good, they're blowing up the town with paranormal energy."

"I don't suppose they could turn it off?" I asked Harriet. "Or maybe just dial it down a little?"

"That I do not know. I don't personally know any demons. They're very rare." Harriet leaned forward again; her expression sober. "If this demon that has moved into your area is truly evil, bad things will follow."

That didn't sound good.

"Can you define *bad things*?" Missy asked, chewing on her lower lip. "Are we talking death or just a little rotten weather?"

"It depends on the demon. Everyone may simply have terrible luck, the skies will turn gray, and all hope will be lost. That's the best-case scenario."

She paused dramatically, and I found that I was holding my breath.

"And the worst?" Missy prompted. "What's the worst-case scenario?"

"The dead become servants to the demon and then rise up, slaying all of the living. When that happens a portal to the underworld will open and all of those trapped there will be let loose upon the earth."

Swallowing hard, I replayed the words in my head. Bad stuff.

"So you're saying that the ghosts in town will kill all of us and then hell will get a back door into Ravenmist?"

"Yes."

"That wouldn't be good."

"It would be disastrous for all mankind."

I was inexplicably angry at Harriet. How were we just hearing this now?

"Were you planning to tell anyone about this so we could stop it?"

"Other than the energy surge I hadn't seen any signs of evil."

"What signs should we be looking for?" Missy asked, sitting on the edge of her seat, the tea long forgotten. My own had to be colder than ice.

"Plague. Pestilence. Famine. War. Death. You know…the usual."

Missy's head jerked up. "Death? Do you mean death in Ravenmist?"

"Yes, if the death toll should suddenly rise that would be a cause for concern."

I knew what Missy was thinking but four murders in seven months wasn't *that* big of a deal. It was unusual for our town but hardly unprecedented. And there wasn't any plague or famine in sight. We were in the clear. No issues at all.

Right?

"IT'S NOT A big deal," I argued in the car on the way home. "It's four murders. It's a blip. An anomaly. We may go years without another one. And they weren't Ravenmist citizens. They were out of towners."

"She didn't say that only Ravenmist citizens would be victims," Missy pointed out. "But we can't look at only the murders, Tedi. Madame Harriet said *deaths*. We need to look to see if *deaths in general* are going up."

"Well, are they?" I sounded testy because I was. We had a demon in our hometown and frankly, it made me cranky. "You're the Grim Reaper. Have you been busier than usual lately?"

"I've only been the reaper for a few years so it's hard to tell. I don't feel any busier. I could ask my dad. He might see trends that I don't."

"Are you going to tell your family that we have a demon?"

"Of course. Are you going to tell your mom?"

"No."

"No? She knows about ghosts and reapers now. Why wouldn't you tell her?"

"Because there is nothing she could do. It would only scare her."

"Technically, there's nothing we can do."

"Au contraire."

Sighing, Missy pressed a hand to her forehead. "I'm terrified to ask. Just what do you think we can do?"

"Find the demon."

"How? Spill milkshakes on everyone that's moved to town in the last year?" When I didn't answer right away, Missy groaned and shook her head. "That's your plan, isn't it? You're going to spill milk on everyone and see if they give off smoke. Tedi, you can't do that."

That's where my best friend was wrong.

"I think that I can. What are they going to do? Throw me in jail? It's not against the law to spill milk on another person. If they don't burn, we'll apologize profusely and offer to have their clothes dry cleaned. Piece of cake."

"We?" Missy's voice rose an octave. "When did you become we?"

"I can't go around spilling milk on people. You said so yourself. I'll get a reputation for being a butterfingers. It will be much more believable if we both do it. Hey, maybe I should tell my mom after all. She can do it, too. Then people won't go around saying look out for Tedi Hamilton. She can't walk and drink dairy at the same time."

"I'm lactose intolerant," Missy protested. "No one will believe it."

My mind was already whirring, putting together a plan.

"First we'll need to figure out who has moved to town in the last year or so. It can't be that many. Then we'll watch them for awhile. Figure out their habits. No, wait. I'll just invite them all to a dinner at the inn. Some sort of welcome to Ravenmist dinner gift certificate thing."

"And then pour milk on all of them? Sure, no one will notice anything strange about that. Why don't you just fill the swimming pool with milk and throw a pool party?"

"Now you're just being ridiculous. It's not warm enough for a pool party."

Missy scraped her fingers through her long hair. "Tedi, we're in big trouble here. What if we can't find out who the demon is? We can't let all the souls in hell loose on the earth."

"We won't let that happen." I sounded far more confident than I actually felt. "Besides, I'm not ready to die yet. And certainly not at the hands of one of the town ghosts."

It made having one in my bedroom closet a heck of a lot less desirable.

Missy pulled out her phone. "I'm going to call my grandmother. I think we need to bring in the whole family and research this. There has to be some sort of spell or ritual. We have to find an answer."

The fate of the world rested on our shoulders.

No pressure.

Chapter Eight

I STILL HADN'T had a chance to speak with Sasha and I found her sitting on the back patio with a book and a lemonade. She was stretched out on one of our lounge chairs wearing a straw hat to protect her skin from the sun. She was always preaching to me about sunscreen being the key to looking younger.

As a redhead, I'd slathered so much SPF 100 on my skin I ought to look like a toddler.

I held up the plate of petit fours I'd grabbed in the kitchen and watched as her eyes lit up. She tossed her paperback aside and clapped her hands together in glee. She might be watching her figure but she was a sucker for fancy patisserie.

"Tell me there's something chocolate on that plate," she said, scanning the plate's contents when I set it on the small table between us. "Or lemon. I love lemon."

"Chocolate, lemon, coconut, and there's a raspberry here as well, I think. Help yourself."

The dainty treats were bite-sized but like myself, Sasha wanted to make them last, so she took a delicate nibble and then closed her eyes and groaned.

"That's to die for. You have to eat one, too. I can't do this by myself."

"Heck yes, I'm going to eat, too." I bit into the coconut and sighed. "It's like a little plate of heaven. I'm sorry I haven't been around today. It's been a little crazy."

"No worries." Sasha waved away my concerns with a grin. "I've been enjoying the very rare sensation of doing nothing. I used the gym earlier today and now I'm reading, something I haven't done in way too long."

She did not mention Darrell going into her room last night.

"I'm sorry about last night, too. The whole town is a little off balance."

"I went to bed early. I was exhausted." She picked up another treat from the plate. "Seriously, don't worry about entertaining me. I'm fine. I've been on boring movie sets for years. I can always find something to do."

I'd given her the opening and she still didn't mention Darrell. I kind of had a feeling that she wasn't going to. In fact, she was lying to me, something I'd never thought she would do. Why? Did she have something to hide? I knew it wasn't that she was a murderer but now I was curious as to why she felt she couldn't tell me the truth.

But I did remember why I wanted to talk to her last night.

"Last night when I returned to the inn, I saw Bill Warner, Jessica Hornsby, and Laura Mandrell talking together outside. I heard them say that everything was under control and that no one knew what was going on. Or something close to that. I don't suppose you know what they were talking about?"

Sasha's brows shot up and she swallowed the chocolate petit four, her hand over her mouth. "Really? That's very interesting. No, I don't know what they're talking about but it's certainly something to look into. I can see why Laura and Bill would be talking to one another, of course, but Jessica? That's a trio I didn't expect. Did you hear anything else?"

"Just that they shouldn't make any mistakes or it would all be blown out of the water."

Sasha tapped her chin. "Even more interesting. I'm not surprised Laura has a few secrets tucked up her sleeve but I didn't expect it of Jessica. She always seemed so nice and sweet to everybody."

"To be fair, we don't know that she's not nice and sweet," I pointed out. "They could have been talking about something completely innocuous."

Leaning toward me, Sasha kept her voice low. "Or they could be talking about murder."

Whoa. You'd need a pole vault to jump to that conclusion.

"You think they're working together and that they killed Brock? That's...interesting."

She shrugged. "They all had motive, especially Laura. I read the papers this morning. Brock treated everyone like dirt under his feet including his agent and Jessica."

"My customers don't always treat me well but not once have I banded together with a few other people and plotted their demise."

"What do you usually do?"

"Give them extra towels." When Sasha frowned, I explained further. "You know…the old kill them with kindness ploy. It's hard to stay mad with someone who puts chocolate mints on your pillow."

"That's true, but I don't think Brock was the type that cared about extra towels. You should have heard how he spoke to his wife. It was horrible. Like she was his servant. Not once did she ever say anything to him but there were times that if looks could kill…"

"Brock Mandrell would be dead," I finished for her.

"Several times over. I bet she shot him. She'd simply had enough and she killed him. End of story. Now she's free and has the money, too."

"Let's say your theory is true. Why would she bring in other people to her plot? From what I've seen in the movies, the more people that know the quicker you find yourself behind bars."

"She might be planning for one of them to take the fall for her. That's what I'd do. Find others with motive and blame them. Just enough that a jury would have reasonable doubt."

"You've given this a lot of thought."

Laughing, Sasha held up her book. "Not really, but I read mysteries."

"I don't know if you're right but I do hope that Jack catches the killer soon. Having a murderer loose in town isn't good for business in the long run. And it can't be good for you, either. Weren't you supposed to fly to New York tomorrow morning?"

"The meeting was cancelled. Until I'm cleared, I'm persona non grata in the industry."

"Then we need to clear your name as soon as possible."

"It shouldn't be long. I'm telling you...Laura Mandrell is guilty as sin."

Then she was someone that I needed to talk to.

IN THE END, Laura Mandrell found me, not the other way around. I'd been called into my office for a phone call and then I looked up from my desk and there she was. She asked if she could talk to me for a moment and of course I said yes. The universe was clearly giving me a hand today and I fully appreciated it. I could use the help.

She settled into my guest chair and crossed her legs at her ankles. That was a move my mother had tried to teach all of her daughters when we were young. Peggy said it was ladylike and elegant but the problem was that she hadn't given birth to elegant ladylike daughters, except for Amie. My older sister Amie was a real pain. She was all about being a lady and I'd leave her to it. She was also the most emotional one of us and could cry or scream at the drop of a hat.

"How can I help you, Mrs. Mandrell?"

"Please...just call me Laura." The woman folded her hands together and gave me a tremulous smile. "I'd like to make a statement to the media and I was hoping you could help me organize that."

"Of course. I'll help as much as I can, but I have to admit that I thought you already did."

Her lips twisted and fingers tightened until the knuckles turned white. "That was Brock's agent that made the statement for me. And then Brock's publicist made one. Once again, for me. Frankly, I'm tired of other people talking for me. I'd like to speak for myself."

Alrighty then.

"I can get in touch with Gus. He runs the local paper. Were you thinking of just speaking to one reporter or having a press conference?"

"A press conference, please. That way I can answer everyone's questions. I have nothing to hide."

I wasn't about to comment on her last statement. She had, however, made it with such ferocity that I was inclined to believe her. Had she convinced Jack as well? And where was he? Usually he was camped in my kitchen eating free food. What was going on with him lately? Was it... Cara?

"We've had press conferences here at the inn in the past. We usually do them on the back patio area if the weather is good. If not, we can do it in the lobby."

Sadly, the conference center that was being worked on wasn't ready yet. I was having one of the outbuildings renovated but it would be a few months before the work was done.

"I'll call Gus and get him working on it." My hand hovered above the phone on my desk. "I can't imagine that it was easy to be married to someone so famous."

"The fame wasn't the problem," Laura sighed. "It was Brock. He wasn't a good person. When I first met him, I was dazzled by his charm and talent but after we were married, he didn't bother with that anymore. He could be cold and cruel, and a shameless womanizer. He had affairs all throughout our marriage. He had one with your friend Sasha while we filmed the movie."

"Are you sure?" I croaked, my fingers wrapping around the receiver of the phone. "Did you...catch them together?"

The way Sasha spoke of Brock it was hard to believe that she'd ever had an affair with him. This couldn't be true.

Laura just laughed. "I didn't have to. She spent more time in Brock's trailer than she did her own. I was married to Brock Mandrell a long time and I know the signs. But she found out what everyone has learned the hard way. Brock was about Brock. Exclusively. If she thought he was going to help her career she was sadly mistaken. After all, he never helped mine. Once we were married, he made sure I never landed another role ever again."

"I didn't realize you were an actress."

"It was a long time ago. Brock promised to help make me a star, but that was all a ruse. Frankly, he didn't like any competition for attention. He loved the spotlight more than he ever loved me."

He'd certainly jumped into it fast enough at the morgue.

"I know what people are saying," Laura went on. "They think I killed him for the money. But I didn't have to. I had a good lawyer and he said that the prenup wasn't worth the paper it was printed on."

I didn't know much about divorce settlements between wealthy people. My ex David and I split the proceeds from a condo sale. We'd always had separate bank accounts so there wasn't much to fight over.

"I'm sure people don't think you killed your husband," I replied in my best soothing tone. "People don't even believe what they read in the paper anymore."

Laura leaned forward, a small smile playing on her lips. "People want to believe the worst in others I've found, so you bet they believe what they read. I've seen how people look at me today and no one thinks I'm a grieving widow. Your sheriff certainly doesn't believe it."

Ah yes, Jack. Where was he? It looked like I was going to have to do his job for him.

"Where were you when Brock was killed?" I asked, keeping my tone casual. As if I didn't care at all. "If you have an alibi, it doesn't matter what anyone believes."

"I'd stepped outside to take a call. And no – before you ask – I don't know if anyone saw me. So I don't have a strong alibi."

"I'm sure they'll find the real killer soon and you'll be cleared."

Unless it really was Laura. I wasn't too sure about her yet.

"I hope so. This whole situation has been so stressful and I do feel a little guilty."

"Guilty? Why?"

"Because I hated my husband and I'm not sorry he's dead. In fact, when your sheriff finds the real killer, I may take some of Brock's millions and get him a good lawyer. I'm sure they had a good reason for killing him."

That was...blunt. And honest. And...just wow. Okey-dokey.

"You probably shouldn't do that. In fact, you shouldn't tell anyone that you're not sorry he's dead."

"That would make me a liar."

"That's better than being on trial for murder. Until they arrest someone, you might want to keep those thoughts on the down low."

"Are you going to tell the sheriff?"

Was I?

"Because you don't need to bother. I already told him. Funny, he said the same thing that you did. That I should probably keep that to myself. The fact is that everyone who ever met Brock Mandrell came to hate him eventually. There's a long list of suspects and the cops better bring in reinforcements because it's going to take an army to go through them all. A lot of people are happier now that he's dead."

If that was true – and Laura wasn't the killer – which one of those people pulled the trigger? Or did Laura do it and was simply trying to throw everyone off?

I really needed to talk to Jack.

Chapter Nine

NOT WASTING ANOTHER minute, I headed out of the inn and down the street to the sheriff's office. It was a sunny day and uncharacteristically warm for this early in the season. Everyone I passed on the sidewalk had a smile on their face and a spring in their step. It was good to see that the town wasn't letting a murder bring down their mood. The citizens of Ravenmist were nothing if not resilient.

I was in front of The Grateful Raven when the door to the sheriff's office swung open and Jack stepped out, followed by Cara. They were both laughing and smiling.

Let me repeat that in case you didn't hear me in the cheap seats.

Jack Garrett was laughing and smiling. That wasn't his usual behavior, and that was a major understatement. Jack liked to scowl and glower, look down at others with a superior attitude. Smiles and chuckles? That wasn't the man I'd come to know.

He must really like Cara.

And that was fine. Just fine. I was happy for him. It was good to see someone who was normally so unhappy be…happier. I watched as they walked down the block, chatting as if they'd known one another for years instead of days.

"It's not too late, you know."

I turned around to see Daisy standing in the doorway of the diner.

"Too late for what?"

She nodded toward the end of the block. "The sheriff. That woman isn't going to stay in Ravenmist."

"That's too bad then because they clearly like each other."

"It's okay to be jealous."

No. No, it wasn't. I'd predicated my entire life on not wanting what other people had and I wasn't about to change now.

"I am not jealous. I am not the jealous type."

"That's true," Daisy conceded. "Okay, you're not jealous, but I do think you're a little put out about it all. He's not showing you as much attention since she came to town."

"I do not need his attention. I'm not a cocker spaniel."

I was fine on my own. I had a great life, lots of friends. I was happy, gosh darn it.

"She'll leave and it will all go back to the way it was. Or you could put your foot down finally and make some progress in your relationship. I swear the two of you are taking your own sweet time about it all. Neither of you are getting any younger."

"That's just what a girl wants to hear, Daisy. That's she's getting old."

"A slice of pie might make you feel better."

"Make it coconut and I'm in."

Daisy opened the door wider. "Then you better get in here. I'll get your pie. Coffee, too?"

"I wouldn't say no."

In fact, I'd never say no to Daisy's delicious coffee. I think she put cinnamon in it.

In record time I had a huge slab of pie and a cup of coffee in front of me. Daisy had slid into the booth to keep me company, sipping on her iced tea and picking at a cinnamon Danish.

"Jack and I do not have a relationship," I said after a few bites of coconut custard and meringue heaven. "We're only friends."

"Okay, your *friend* is walking down the street with another woman. Are you sure it doesn't bother you? Just a little?"

Was I bothered? It wasn't my habit to deny my feelings. When my ex had asked me for a divorce, I hadn't pretended I wasn't angry and a little hurt. I'd tried hard to make my marriage work and I felt like a failure for awhile. I'd admitted all of that easily, not wanting to pretend that everything was fine. Eventually it did become fine, of course, and that anger was replaced with resolve. I didn't want to go through all of that again.

"Mostly it surprises me. He's as adamant as I am about not wanting romance. I guess...I guess I miss having him be cynical with me."

It was kind of comforting to know that he and I were in the same place with the same attitude. Now it felt like he'd...moved on. Did that mean I was standing still?

Daisy nodded in understanding. "It was something you both had in common. I'm sure you have other things in common, too."

Other than a deep love of food, I wasn't sure if we did.

And I wasn't sure why it mattered. Had we truly…become friends? We'd been playing at it sort of half-heartedly but had it happened when I wasn't looking? Was I – egads – fond of Jack? Would I miss him if he wasn't here?

Shockingly, I think so.

"He was my friend," I muttered under my breath before shoving another bite into my mouth. The sugar from the pie was beginning to hum through my veins. Delicious.

"As you know, we all think you should be more than that," Daisy said. "But friends isn't a bad start."

"I don't want to be in love. It's messy and inconvenient. And let's face it, Jack would be a pain of a boyfriend." I slapped the table with the flat of my hand and a few heads whipped around at the sound. "And let's talk about that word. Boyfriend. I'm over thirty, Daisy. I can't have a boyfriend because I don't want a boy. But man friend sounds wrong. See? I can't date or have romance because I wouldn't know what to call the man in my life."

Chuckling, Daisy shook her head. "How about *husband*?"

I swear my heart stopped in my chest for a moment before starting up again.

"Don't scare me like that. I need a husband like I need a hole in my head. It's one thing to have a romantic relationship but it's entirely more serious to speak of marriage. It's an institution, Daisy, and one should be wary if you're about to be institution-alized."

"You have major commitment issues."

"I don't consider them issues. I like to think of them as assets."

"While you're doing that, Jack is with that woman."

I shoved the last bite of pie into my mouth.

"The thing is, I like Cara. She's really nice. Jack could do a lot worse."

Now I sounded like everyone else in Ravenmist. If you can't beat 'em, join 'em.

"At least you're not feeling sorry for yourself."

I pushed my plate away and picked up my coffee cup. I already had a plan and it was a great one. Fabulous. Epic. "Once again, I'm not the type. In fact, you know what we need, Daisy? We need a girls' night out. You, me, Missy, maybe some fattening food and several romantic comedies. What do you say?"

Daisy clapped her hands together in delight, her expression gleeful. "That sounds like a perfect idea. In fact, let's turn it into a bachelorette party for Amelia. We can have food, music, movies, and dancing. This is so exciting. I can't wait to tell her. We can do it right here. I'll close a little early. This is going to be so much fun! What a great idea, Tedi."

Wait...what?

My girls' night out had just turned into a bachelorette party.

For a hundred-year-old plus ghost.

Just another day in Ravenmist. I'd better call Missy and tell her the news.

DID YOUR MOM ever make you go somewhere you didn't particularly want to go with the dubious argument that it would be all fun and games once you got there? So you did go and you didn't have any fun at all? In fact, the entire evening was a snooze?

That was this party. And apparently it was all my idea.

At least that's what Daisy had told Amelia, Missy, and my mother. To be fair, they appeared to be much more excited about the festivities than I was. Missy was in charge of the music and my mother had lent a helping hand with the decorations. She'd also worked on the entertainment and thank goodness I'd been able to talk her out of the stripper she'd wanted to hire. Once I pointed out that Amelia was really a teenager from another century and it wouldn't be appropriate, she'd immediately backed down.

It did, however, remind me of my own bachelorette party that my sisters had thrown when I married David. To my utter horror, my *mother* had attended and to make a long, agonizing story a heck of a lot shorter, we all ended up at the library. What a wild night that was.

Not.

I was home by ten-thirty.

The food was amazing and Daisy had outdone herself in that department. She'd somehow managed to throw together a buffet of yummy dishes and I wasn't too proud to fill my plate. Missy was playing some tunes from the eighties and my mother was telling the story of when she and my dad went to see the rock band Boston in concert. Amelia, of course, had a lot of questions including *what's a rock band?*

I'd staked out a spot in a booth and was currently stuffing my face as if I hadn't eaten in weeks when Amelia slid across from me, her face wreathed in smiles. Both she and Charles were a heck of a lot happier now that they lived with Daisy than when they'd been alone by the lake.

"Thank you for having this party for me, Tedi."

I couldn't possibly tell her that I'd been planning a girls' night out, not a girls' and ghouls' night out. But I also didn't want to take credit for something that I didn't do.

"It was really Daisy's idea. I was suggesting a night out and she thought to amp it up to a party."

"It's still quite thoughtful."

Did you hear that, Mom? I was thoughtful.

"I hope you're enjoying it."

Because it would be a shame if no one was having a good time.

"I am. This is a completely new tradition. In my day, we would have made a quilt."

On the scales of life, with one side of music and food while the other was sewing a quilt, I know which I'd go for every time.

"That sounds like a lovely tradition as well."

"It is but we really have no need of one now, although Daisy has decorated our rooms upstairs quite nicely and Missy lets us borrow books from her store."

I may not have mentioned that Charles had befriended Edward, Missy's ghost in her bookstore, and Terrence from my own closet. Charles was fascinated by modern technology and the other two young men were happy to teach him all about it and bring him up to date. Amelia, on the other hand, liked to sit in Missy's bookstore and read crime novels about serial killers. I wasn't sure how to feel about that so I ignored it.

"So are you nervous about getting married?"

I have no clue why I asked that. It was just something that popped out of my mouth. I'd sure been asked it plenty of times on the run up to my wedding.

Side note...I was nervous as all get out before my wedding and I should have listened to that little voice in the back of my head that was telling me to run for my life.

But I digress.

Amelia gave me that gentle smile I'd seen so many times and shook her head. "Not in the least. I've loved Charles for so long it seems only natural to finally get married. That's what we've wanted from the beginning but our families were against it."

Just in case you're not up on Charles and Amelia's tragic love story turned happily ever after, they were crazy in love teenagers in 1874 but their families were against the match. Fast forward and the couple decided to drown themselves in Ravenmist Lake so they couldn't be separated by their parents. They became known as the Young Lovers and for over a hundred years had bickered and fought. Then Daisy stepped in and convinced them to move in with her and now it was all hearts and flowers.

I didn't comment on how "natural" it was for two ghosts to tie the knot. They were happy and that was good enough for me.

"I'm really happy for both of you."

Amelia's smile fell and she suddenly looked so sad. "Thank you so much, Tedi. I was so sorry to hear about the sheriff courting another girl."

You know gossip in town is bad when even the dead hear about it.

"It's fine. He and I are just friends."

Frowning, she shook her head. "I'm not familiar with how that would work. You're friends with the sheriff but not in love?"

I suppose in her century that didn't happen too often. "Just pals. Buddies. Not romantic in the least. I'm really okay with him going out with someone else. It's all fine."

In fact, the more I'd thought about it today the better I was with it all. Jack and I would never have been able to make a relationship work – not that I was trying to go that direction. We were both far too snarky and cynical. Cara was a better match for him because she was sweet and nice while I was…difficult. He was no day at the beach, either.

"You're so brave," Amelia sighed. "You're not scared to be alone. I'd never want that."

Those words perked me up a bit. Because I wasn't afraid to be on my own. In fact, most of the time I preferred it.

"That's true. I'm okay with it."

Amelia glanced over her shoulder and then pointed to the door to the upstairs. "Do you see that? They say women need men but it's really the other way around. Men need us. That's what my mother always said. Just look at them. They could be doing anything tonight but they're spying on us."

Indeed, Amelia wasn't wrong. Three heads were peering around the door trying to see what was going on – Charles, Edward, and Terrence. Daisy had seen them too and was bustling over there to shoo them away.

"Charles didn't get a party of his own?"

"He said he wanted Edward and Terrence to come over. They're playing with the computer again." She frowned and tossed a glare toward her intended. "I don't like that thing. It makes so much noise."

I had a sneaking suspicion that our friendly ghosts had discovered YouTube and video games in addition to the documentary they were making about the in-between.

The music changed from a peppy pop tune to a slightly slower country song. I groaned when I recognized it, slumping down in the booth seat a little hoping my mother wouldn't see me. They'd played this song at my sister's wedding and made me line dance to it.

Sadly, I didn't have any luck tonight. My mother grinned and threw her hands up in the air, doing a few steps on the tile floor.

"C'mon, Tedi. You know this dance."

I prayed for lightning to strike me but it must have been busy elsewhere.

"Mom," I whined, shrinking farther back in the seat. "I don't wanna."

My mother rolled her eyes and then held out her hand. To Amelia.

"Would you like me to teach you the dance? It's a lot of fun."

Amelia nodded vigorously. "I would, thank you. This is so much fun. Thank you for the party, Tedi."

"You're welcome," I replied automatically, once again getting credit where it wasn't deserved.

Amelia hopped onto the small dance floor where several tables used to reside but had been pushed aside for tonight. Missy stood next to her and began to teach her the steps. My mother, on the other hand, was still looking at me with a scowl on her face.

"You're about as much fun as the flu," she finally said, her hands on her hips. That's when I knew she was serious. "If you're upset about Jack—"

"I'm not."

"I heard that he and that woman are at the Raven's Wing tonight."

The gossip in this town was second to none.

"Then I'm glad for him. I'm not looking for love, Mom. If

Jack is, then more power to him."

But it was kind of sad to have lost my partner in cynicism. Egads, would he be...*happy* all the time now? That was a disturbing thought.

"I don't want you to be alone, Tedi."

My mother sounded sad at the thought but it didn't sound to me to be that dire of a situation.

"There are worse things. Being with the wrong person, for example."

"True, but you won't know they're right or wrong unless you give them a chance. Open your heart a little. I hate to think that David made you this way. It's like he's won the battle and the war."

Whoa. Just hold the phone. David didn't win anything. He didn't...

Okay, maybe...just maybe...I was letting him get into my head a bit.

"It's good to be cautious."

"It's even better to experience life fully." She pointed to Amelia who was doing a darn good Electric Slide, for someone who was born in the nineteenth century. "Amelia is more alive than you are. What does that say to you?"

If my mother expected me to answer her she didn't wait around for it, instead joining Daisy, Missy, and Amelia on the dance floor. They were laughing and giggling while stepping on each other's toes.

They were having fun. Was I too cool to do that? Had I been

so busy being fine that I'd forgotten to let loose a little? Was I really less alive than the ghosts around me?

Sliding out of the booth, I quickly took stock of my life. The good, the bad, and the ghostly. No way was I going to let a specter live better than me.

Time to put on my boogie shoes. Watch out, world. I'm going to dance.

It wasn't exactly earth shattering, but it was a start.

Chapter Ten

LAURA MANDRELL WAS dressed in a modest navy blue suit and matching high heels for her press conference the next morning. Her hair was perfectly styled and her makeup impeccable. The kind of makeup that you can't really see but your gut tells you is there because no one on this earth could have skin that flawless.

I'd gone up to her room to briefly check on her and she was practicing her statement in the mirror while Bill Warner the agent barked orders into the phone to some poor human being who should have hung up on him. I didn't even pretend to understand Hollywood. Instead, I wished her well and told her that everything was ready for the top of the hour. She gave me a dazzling smile and a thumbs up.

She was also not nervous in the least, which sort of surprised me because there was a hoard of press on my back patio waiting to make her the biggest story of the news day. There were press trucks from all over, including the major news networks, and so far, they'd trampled my lawn with their tires, drank gallons of coffee, eaten dozens of donuts, and generally made a nuisance of themselves.

I'd always been a big fan of the free press but right now they could sit down and behave themselves. I'd caught one of them hanging out in my pantry hoping to catch candid photos of someone famous. I'd pulled him out of there by his ear and given him a lecture about trespassing. There was another one that tried to hide behind a maid's housekeeping cart, but I'd dragged him outside as well. I was doing a heck of a job, channeling my inner *Roadhouse*.

Gus, the guy that ran the local paper had set all of this up, and I was still in a state of disbelief how quickly it had come together and how many people had shown up on such short notice. One of them was sitting in my kitchen drinking coffee and eating a ham and cheese omelet.

I nodded coolly to him as I filled my mug with coffee. It was only my second cup of the day. I'd been too busy wrangling paparazzi to get my full caffeine fix.

"Jack."

"Tedi."

He scooped another forkful of fluffy eggs into his mouth and hummed in appreciation. My chef was amazing and could turn a simple dish into poetry.

"I'm surprised to see you here. You've been quite busy."

I sounded like I cared which is exactly what I didn't want.

"I have been working on a murder case." He took the last bite of omelet and then set his fork on the plate. "It has been busy, though. I wish I could say that I'm close to making an arrest."

"You have lots of suspects."

He nodded, dabbing at his mouth with a paper napkin. "Too many, if you ask me. Everyone hated Brock Mandrell's guts. They all had motive."

I hated myself for asking but I couldn't stop myself.

"Anyone that stands out?"

"Not really. That's why I'm here today."

"I'm not sure I follow your logic."

"The wife of the deceased is giving a press conference today. I'd say that was a good reason for being here. I want to hear what she has to say."

"Have you been able to rule out anyone?"

"Jessica Hornsby, the director's assistant. There are several witnesses that place her in the theater at the time of death. And of course, Cara Lassiter. You were able to give her an alibi."

"I didn't know that Jessica was off the list."

I did know that he'd been at the pub with Cara last night. But I didn't mention that.

"That's recent. It's taken quite awhile to do all the interviews and piece them together. I'm a deputy short this week. Dale is on vacation."

"That's why you've been so busy?"

I really needed to learn to keep my mouth shut. I just couldn't let it go.

Rubbing his chin, he sighed. "This case and another project. Apparently, Cara Lassiter is going to play a cop in a television show and she asked me to help coach her a little for the role. I'm not sure I'm really the person to do it but somehow I found myself saying yes despite having a dozen good reasons not to do it."

It was as if someone had thrown a spanner into the wheels of my brain. I couldn't quite wrap my head around his words.

"You were helping Cara? For a role?"

He nodded, taking a sip of his steaming coffee. "I've answered about a million of her questions and let her sit in the station asking my deputies a million more. Hopefully we're done because I told her I couldn't allow her to impede this investigation."

He'd been helping her for a part in a television show. That's it.

"Has she?"

That made him smile but it was his usual cynical one, not one of happiness. "Now, Tedi, when have I ever had an issue telling someone no?"

"Never, but you could have had a sudden personality change."

"I doubt that would ever happen."

I felt an irrational rush of joy run through me. Jack was still Jack. There was comfort in that. But was I the same? After last night, I'd vowed to open up a little more. Let myself be happy and not worry so much about it being taken away.

"Personally, I'm turning over a new leaf," I said proudly. "I'm going to be more optimistic and less jaded."

Apparently, I'd said something absolutely hilarious because Jack threw his head back and laughed until there were tears coming out of his eyes. He wiped at them and coughed a few times before he could speak again.

"You're going to be more optimistic? I honestly can't wait to see how this looks, Tedi. Are you going to start reciting affirmations in the mirror in the morning? *I'm worthy. I'm happy. People don't make me mad. I don't care if that guy cuts me off in traffic.*"

"Haha, very funny. No, I am not going to do that. I'm simply going to try and see the brighter side of situations more often. I think I expect the worst a little too much, and I don't want to be like that. You know...baby steps."

"Baby steps," Jack repeated. "That's a good plan. Take it slow. We wouldn't want to shock your system or anything. What's brought on this miraculous change of heart, may I ask?"

"I was hanging out with Daisy, Missy, and my mom last night—"

"I heard about that."

The question was, did he hear all of it? Like how it was a party for a soon-to-be wed ghost? Doubtful.

"You did?"

"Of course, Daisy's is only two doors down from the station and she closed up early for a so-called private event."

"It was sort of a girls' night out. Just some food and music. Nothing too crazy."

"I knew that as well. We didn't get any disturbing the peace calls about it. It was the party that has you turning over a new leaf? Must have been some bash. At least no one ended up dead."

I gave him my best mean look. "Listen, wise guy, you could be more optimistic too. You're practically a raincloud in every room you walk in."

"That's because I'm a cop," he replied promptly and with a smile. "I've seen the seedy underbelly of life so I have a good reason not to be a ray of sunshine. What's your excuse?"

The answer popped out of my mouth before I could stop it.

"I was born this way."

"Then good luck changing. And I know my opinion probably doesn't count for much, but I don't see why you would want to change. There's nothing wrong with the way you are. You're basically a nice, helpful person but you don't take any guff. That's nothing to be ashamed of."

"Careful, you almost said something nice about me."

"I thought we were becoming friends. Friends say nice things about each other, and compared to me you're a raging optimist." He leaned forward and raised his brows. "And what would you say about me, Tedi?"

What would I say?

"You're very…efficient."

Chuckling, he stood and gathered up his keys, stuffing them into his pocket. "I'll take it, especially as I pride myself on my efficiency. Now isn't it time for the press conference?"

It was and thank goodness. I don't think I could take one more minute of this conversation.

LOOKING EVEN CALMER than the last time I'd seen her, Laura Mandrell stood up in front of dozens of reporters, including Gus from our very own local paper, and finally spoke for herself. No agent, no publicist. Just her and in her own words.

"First of all, I want to thank all of you for the outpouring of love and support I've received since Brock's tragic and untimely passing. It's been so much easier traveling down this path knowing that you are all with me. I'm so humbled and grateful."

"Second, I wanted to thank the police force of Ravenmist. They've shown nothing but pure professionalism and an unending drive to find the heinous person who committed this horrible deed. I have complete confidence that they will make an arrest soon."

Jack's brows shot up in surprise. Clearly, he hadn't known she was going to say that. Now the pressure was really on.

"I also want all of you to know that I won't let what's happened–"

"I did it!"

A voice came from the back of the rows of press. A young woman dressed in jeans and a white blouse jumped up and began racing down the aisle, a gun in her hand pointed directly at Laura Mandrell.

"I did it! And you're next!"

Chapter Eleven

JACK'S DEPUTIES IMMEDIATELY tackled the woman to the ground, separating her from her weapon before cuffing and dragging her kicking and screaming into my sitting room. The press was in an uproar, trying to film the confession and follow the deputies but Jack was having none of that. He'd pushed back the reporters and practically snarled at them to stay outside before posting two deputies at the door to make sure they obeyed.

And me?

At first, I'd tried to calm down the press but was practically trampled on. I kept telling them to sit down and be patient but they simply shoved me out of the way. Finally, I threw myself in front of Laura and backed her into the inn. My assistant manager bustled her into my office which had a lock on the door.

It was complete mayhem. I heard Jack on the phone calling in every part-time deputy in Ravenmist along with the fire department, and the county and state police. It had only been a few minutes and I could already hear sirens in the distance.

The press wasn't about to give in and they'd rounded the side of the inn and were now pounding on my front door and looking in the windows, screaming and yelling that I was violating the free press. Thank goodness the front desk clerk had the foresight to lock it. There were still other entrances and I had employees scurrying around trying to shore up our defenses. It was as if this was the Alamo and we were under siege.

And we all know how it ended at the Alamo.

Honestly, I wasn't sure my doors and windows would hold up against the tidal wave of reporters that desperately wanted inside. There was a big story going on in my drawing room and they wanted a piece of it, even if it meant battering down the walls of a structure more than a hundred years old.

I was staring down at the floor when a set of highly shined black shoes came into my line of sight.

Jack.

"Are you okay?"

Looking up, I rubbed at my temples where a loo-loo of a headache was beginning to form.

"I don't know." I nodded toward the sitting room. "Shouldn't you be in there?"

"I figured I'd better make sure you were okay. She hasn't said anything except that she did it and that the wife was next. She keeps repeating it over and over. I'm going to take her to the station and question her once she calms down a little. I'm also going to get her firearm to the lab and see if it's our murder weapon."

"Well...Laura did say you'd be making an arrest very soon."

Blowing out a breath, Jack shook his head. "I know this is going to sound cynical and you're trying to be optimistic and all but I wouldn't put it past these Hollywood types to plant her in the audience to get a story."

Heavens to Betsy.

"Jack, you may have hit the pinnacle of cynicism. That would be simply awful."

"I don't like thinking it. It just seems too easy."

"Maybe you're due for an easy win."

"Maybe. Listen, don't worry about security for the inn. I'll make sure you and your guests are safe. If I take our suspect to the station that should take some of the heat off of you."

"Thank you."

My phone vibrated in my pocket and I almost jumped out of my skin when I felt it. I'd completely forgotten about it which would have been a first for me. Jack politely retreated back into the drawing room with a nod, leaving me to take my call. The display read *Missy*. She'd probably heard what had happened and she was worried about me.

"I'm okay," I answered. "No injuries or anything. Jack has it all under control."

"Uh...that's great. I guess. Why would you be injured?"

She hadn't heard. Even the gossip mill in Ravenmist couldn't work in six minutes.

"The press conference got exciting. I thought you were calling to make sure I was okay."

"I definitely want to hear about it then, but I'm actually calling about our other project. You know I've been looking through books, right? I think I've found one that might help us."

"I want to hear about it."

Looking around the inn, though, I couldn't abandon it until the situation was under control and a heck of a lot calmer.

"I just can't leave right now. This place is total chaos. The press has lost their minds and any sense of civilized behavior. They're trying to break down my doors."

"Ahhh, that's the pounding I hear in the background. It sounds a little like a hammer."

"It wouldn't shock me if they were using one to take the door off the hinges."

"Your door hinges are inside, not outside."

"Then they're removing the windows."

"Maybe I should come over there then."

"Use the secret entrance."

Few people knew that the barn was connected to the basement by a tunnel. Missy and I had played down there when we were kids and before we truly understood the meaning of the word *creepy*. Now I avoided the damp, musty tunnel as much as possible.

"I'll be there in ten."

Hopefully, Missy had found the answer we needed.

"SO JACK HAS the killer in custody?" Missy asked. We'd tucked ourselves away in my apartment now that the area was secure. Jack had deputies posted on all corners of the inn even though most of the press had followed him to the sheriff's station. Just as he'd predicted.

"Some woman confessed and then threatened Laura Mandrell that she was next, so I guess the answer is yes. He, of course, thinks that it's just too easy so he's suspicious of it."

"It can't be often that a killer confesses in front of a crowd of people."

"And on camera," I added. "There were plenty of those there."

"So much drama. I'm just relieved that you're not hurt."

"Not from lack of trying on their part. A few reporters tried to run me over as they stampeded toward the door. Luckily, I'm nimble."

"Where's Laura Mandrell now?"

"In her room but she said that she might change hotels since they know she's here. I can't say that I blame her."

Missy frowned. "What about Sasha? Where was she during all of this?"

"Thankfully not here. She and Cara went into Spring Bell to do some shopping. She sent me a text this morning. Bless her, she knows that it's been crazy here and she's managed to keep herself busy and occupied."

"Is she still worried about Jack?"

"He hasn't questioned her since that first day. Personally, I think he has bigger fish to fry. But technically she's still a suspect. I'm going to try and have dinner with her tonight."

Missy hefted the heavy and dusty book she'd had tucked under her arm onto my coffee table. "Then let's get to this now."

Wrinkling my nose at the mildew smell coming from the yellowed pages, I peered over Missy's shoulder as she opened the book. It only took a moment for her to locate what she was looking for.

"Here. Right here. It talks about benevolent demons."

"Benevolent demons," I repeated. "Sounds like an oxymoron. Like jumbo shrimp."

"There are such beings, believe it or not. They aren't many of them but they are all over the earth to protect humanity, mostly from ourselves. Physically, they look like humans. A doctor wouldn't even be able to tell the difference, but they're intelligent and physically strong with a great deal of endurance. But the real difference is that they have a different kind of soul from a human. In fact, whether they're good or evil, that's really the only difference. What kind of soul they were given at birth."

"Given?"

Missy shrugged. "They aren't specific about the process. It's more of a fate thing. Whichever family you're born into. Good or evil. The luck of the draw. The book mentions that it's their destiny."

I wasn't a huge believer in destiny. I'd been brought up to believe that people make their own way in life and weren't at the whims of some invisible hand.

"Does it mention how to identify a demon?"

"It does, and according to this book what Madame Harriet told us isn't true. Demons have evolved over the years and spilled milk doesn't make them smoke anymore."

Figures.

"That's great. Then how are we going to figure out who the demon is in Ravenmist? And what else was Madame Harriet wrong about? Maybe everything?"

I wasn't seeing how this book was going to be of any help to us. And make no mistake, we definitely needed all the assistance we could get. Us and… all of humanity.

"They've evolved so that we can't tell. That was the whole point of evolving."

This conversation was becoming more depressing with every passing moment.

"Bottom line it for me, Missy. Is there any good news in that book?"

She pointed to a passage. "There is. Right here. Stay with me because this gets a little convoluted and I'm going to put this in my own words. When the universe was created good and evil were in balance, one not any stronger than the other. Each side was given a certain amount of energy or power, if you will. All evil demons share one basket of energy, and all good demons share their own basket – for want of a better term. Remember, it's all about balancing the scales. Because there are fewer good demons than bad ones, they therefore have excess energy. More energy per demon. Do you follow me?"

No...

"If I say no, will you think I'm stupid?"

"No, because it took awhile for me to get it today. Think about it this way, the chances of our demon being good is quite high because he or she has so much excess energy that they're giving it to the town."

Actually, I kind of did this time.

"So the demons share a pie of energy and if there are only four good demons and ten evil ones then the four get a bigger share of their apple pie than the evil ones do of their peach pie. Like that?"

Missy nodded approvingly. "That's it. But there's more. And it's kind of the bad news."

Oh goody. Bad news. We can never get enough of that.

"This is sort of messing with my resolution to be more optimistic, Missy."

"I know and I'm really sorry about that. I think you have permission to be sarcastic and cynical about this. I'm not feeling all rainbows and kitten whiskers myself."

"Said the Grim Reaper."

"Evil demons don't like good demons. No surprise there. But here's the kicker. If they hunt them down, they can steal that piece of the good-demon-energy-pie and add it to the evil-demon-energy-pie. So for centuries good and evil have hunted each other, stealing energy back and forth trying to get an advantage in the oldest battle in the world. And this is the bad part..."

What? We hadn't arrived there yet? Color me shocked.

"Okay…? I'm ready for the bad part."

"From what I can tell from my reading, Ravenmist is ground zero for the next big war."

This was why resolutions were a pain. Can I be pessimistic now?

Chapter Twelve

WITH THOUGHTS OF a global apocalypse on my mind, it was surprisingly easy to get a good night's sleep. I was exhausted from the day and I was asleep a few minutes after my head hit the pillow. It wasn't as easy to drag myself out of bed the next morning but I'd scheduled breakfast with Sasha. To help myself wake up I took a scalding hot shower and started drinking coffee before I even hit the dining room.

Sasha was already sitting at a table, but she wasn't bright-eyed and bushy-tailed.

"Are you...hungover?" I asked as I sat down across from her. "What did you do last night? I thought you went shopping with Cara."

Taking a drink from her black coffee, Sasha sighed heavily and rubbed at her chin. "We did and then we decided to have dinner at this cute little pub. Next thing I knew we were dancing on the bar and doing shots. It was intense. I haven't cut loose like that in so long. I had to drag Cara out of bed this morning. We didn't get in until about four. We just really wanted to celebrate that I'm no longer a murder suspect."

"Some people just eat chocolate."

"We did that, too." She picked up the menu and began to peruse it. I already knew what I wanted. It was a waffle kind of day. If humanity might not survive, I might as well forget about losing those last five pounds and enjoy myself. "I need to hurry and eat. Cara and I need to be on the road to the airport in forty-five minutes."

Airport? Forty-five minutes?

"You're leaving?"

Not my brightest moment. She wouldn't have mentioned the airport if she wasn't making a break for it.

She gave me her most dazzling Hollywood smile. "The meeting in New York is back on now that everyone knows that I'm not a homicidal maniac. Cara's going with me for a few weeks until she begins shooting a pilot in Los Angeles. She's playing a cop. She even managed to get your sheriff to coach her a little bit. Did I mention that to you? I meant to."

No, and I could have used a head's up. I'd actually thought Jack might be turning into a romantic.

Silly me.

"I'll miss you. Keep in touch."

She reached across the table and grabbed my hand. "You're not getting rid of me so easily. I'm so grateful by how you stood by me these last few days. You're a true friend, Tedi. I'll definitely keep in touch and let's schedule a trip for you to L.A. I want you to visit me for a change. You'll love it there."

Me in La La Land? Stranger things have happened.

"I'll hold you to it. Do you think I could get to meet George Clooney?"

"Girlfriend, the minute I meet you, you'll meet him."

"Deal. And I always knew you couldn't have killed Brock Mandrell. It was a no-brainer."

I didn't mention Laura's assertion that Sasha had been having an affair with her husband. I didn't believe it but even if it were true, it was none of my business. As for Darrell Kennedy visiting her room late at night, that wasn't my business either. Sasha was a grown woman and her life didn't need me judging it.

"Not everyone would have been as kind. Now...what can I order that doesn't have carbs?"

"Bacon. I'll order it too so you won't feel alone."

If humanity might end, I might as well have a pork product to go with my waffles.

If we managed to save the world, however, I was going to need a treadmill.

So for the next approximately forty minutes we chatted, ate, and promised to keep in touch. It wasn't easy as we were both busy but we were determined to try. I even promised to make a visit to L.A. to see her.

I'd barely waved goodbye to Sasha and Cara as they drove away from the inn when I heard a bloodcurdling scream from inside. Dashing up the stairs, I found one of my housekeepers Eleanor standing in the hallway and pointing into one of the rooms and hyperventilating. She kept trying to speak but she just couldn't get the words out. She'd done this once before when there was a huge spider in the bathroom. I couldn't blame her, actually. The eight-legged menace had been a good two inches across and kind of furry. I'd wanted to scream and run too but someone had to kill it.

I'd used a trashcan because I didn't want to ruin my shoes. If I'd had a flamethrower I would have used that, but sadly they were in short supply at a historic inn in the middle of Illinois.

"I got this," I assured her, straightening my shoulders and gritting my teeth. I wasn't going to let an arachnid freak me out.

I grabbed an extra trashcan from her cart and strode into the hotel room. The trick is to act like you don't have any fear even if you're shaking in your boots. Spiders can smell fear. Trust me on this one.

Like a superhero in a movie I was poised and ready to kick some spider patootie with a garbage can in one hand and a roll of paper towels in the other.

Except there was no spider.

Instead, Bill Warner lay face down on the floor in a pool of blood.

I'd picked the wrong day to become an optimist.

JACK WAS NOT in the best of moods. I'd already figured out that murder made him cranky but today he was off the charts. Growling and scowling, he barked orders to his deputies and even people that didn't get a paycheck from him. When he tried to bite my head off, I managed to hold my tongue and simply turned and walked away. Normally, Jack would have let it all alone but not today. He stomped after me all the way to the kitchen muttering something under his breath.

"I'm talking to you."

In a manner of speaking, but not respectfully.

"I'm not listening, Jack. I'm working. You wanted me out of the way and now I am."

The coroner was overseeing the body removal at the moment and I didn't want to hang around for that anyway.

"Why are you acting like a—"

I whirled around and poked a finger in his chest, my own anger beginning to build. "Don't. Just don't. I know what you were about to say and believe me when I tell you that you don't want to do that. This friend thing we're doing can come to an abrupt halt. Just don't."

"There's another dead body, Tedi, and I'm getting tired of it."

In that moment I could see just how exhausted Jack was. Deep lines in his forehead and dark circles under his eyes. He'd aged five years in the last couple of days. All the press attention was beginning to wear on him.

"I don't want this any more than you do. People are going to be afraid to come stay here if this continues."

He was already shaking his head. "This cannot *continue*. We cannot have a body count problem in this town. I won't allow it."

"I don't know how you're going to stop it," I argued. "You had deputies surrounding the inn to keep out the reporters and Bill Warner is still dead."

My usually noisy kitchen was now quieter than a mouse. The entire staff had stopped what they were doing and were staring at us. Like owls. It was disturbing.

"Hey guys, how about you take a little break? Just a few minutes."

Normally my staff would dash for the door but they dragged their feet leaving, lingering to get their phones or a pack of smokes. I even heard my head chef say something about a *lover's quarrel.*

Get real.

Striding over to my pastry area, I cut a huge slab of pie and popped it into the microwave.

"What are you doing?"

Ignoring his question, I dropped two big scoops of vanilla ice cream on the plate when the pie was done warming. Grabbing a fork from a drawer, I slapped the plate down on the counter in front of Jack.

"For all that's good and holy, eat. Please eat."

He opened his mouth to argue but then he snapped it closed, his lips a thin, grim line. Sitting down, he dug into the pie and ice cream with gusto, not saying another word until the plate was empty.

And I mean empty. He practically licked it clean. The man

loved his baked goods.

"That was just what I needed. Thank you."

He wiped at his mouth with a paper napkin I handed him but he didn't sound like the swaggering Jack Garrett that I knew. This one sounded...tired. And fed up.

"Do you want to talk about it?"

As I'd watched Jack eat his pie it had suddenly occurred to me that I was his only friend. Sure, he was friendly with everyone in town – and they all adored him – but he didn't share meals with anyone but me. He didn't share confidences, either. Not that I knew all that much about his personal life but I probably knew more than anyone in town. He was a hard man to get to know, closed off to a certain extent but trying to open up in a place that never heard a secret it didn't want to tell. Bless him, he was doing his best.

"Can I have more pie?"

Heck, yes. I cut another slab that would have satisfied the Jolly Green Giant.

"You don't need to heat it up. I'd eat it out of the pan."

"You don't have to do that."

I gave him a fresh fork. Because I'm weird like that.

He took a few bites and then paused, his gaze far away. "Chelsea Overmeyer didn't kill Brock Mandrell. At least not with the gun that she was threatening Laura Mandrell with."

It took me a moment to realize who Chelsea Overmeyer was.

"Does that mean you have to let her go?"

He shook his head and took another bite. "No, I can hold

her for threatening and stalking Laura Mandrell. According to our now deceased Bill Warner, Chelsea Overmeyer was a well-known whacked-out fan that sent letters and gifts to Brock Mandrell. She's been in and out of...care, and she admitted to me that she's off her meds."

"So maybe she shot him with another gun."

"She admitted that she's not really sure if she killed him or not. If she couldn't have him then no one could. That was her initial explanation of motive but she's all confused. Then I also have eyewitnesses that put her in her hometown of Moline at the time of the murder. Add in the fact that Bill Warner was shot while she was behind bars..."

"So we still don't know for sure who killed Brock Mandrell."

"Or Bill Warner."

It was on the tip of my tongue to tell Jack that this rash of murders was because of demons but he'd only laugh at me and ask if I was off my meds as well. He was the original skeptic. Let's face it, I barely believed it myself.

"That's just at the moment. You'll figure it out. You always do."

"I don't have a murder weapon. I have multiple motives and no witnesses. Now I have a second victim and the killer might or might not be the same person."

Yikes, he thought we had two killers running around Ravenmist?

"You think it was a copycat?"

"I don't know what I think yet."

"So what will you do?"

"What every good cop does. Start from square one and go over the evidence again. Maybe there's something I've missed."

"You'll probably need more pie for that."

"I wouldn't turn it down."

My gut was telling me that his mood was more than simply a difficult case. I'd never seen Jack act like this. There had to be more. What was the worst thing he could do? Yell at me? Pfft, I was used to it by now.

"Something else is bothering you. You wouldn't get this upset about a case."

"What makes you think you know me, Tedi?"

"What makes you think I don't?"

I sounded brave but in reality, I wasn't as sure.

Jack took another bite, chewing thoughtfully. "Don't suppose I could get some coffee to go with this?"

"That could be arranged."

There was always fresh coffee and I filled his cup, sliding it in front of him. He wrapped his hands around it and then finally...*finally*...looked at me.

"Tyler wants to spend the summer with his mom."

I jerked my thumb toward the coffee cup. "Want some whiskey to go with that?"

This time he smiled. "I would love it but I'm on duty."

He took a sip. "I suppose it's a good thing. I don't want him not to be close to his mom."

It was none of my business but he'd opened the door. I

couldn't help but walk through it.

"Does he...see her much or talk to her?"

Jack's lips twisted. "He saw her during Christmas break. He talks to her a few times a week. She's not a bad person."

"That's good, then."

"She's very career focused." He sighed and shoved away the empty plate. "She probably shouldn't have had kids. She loves Tyler a lot and they have a good time when they're together but she's not the type to help him with his homework and make sure he gets to school on time. When he was a baby, she'd get a lot of anxiety when he'd cry and his toddler years stressed her to no end. When we divorced there was no question as to who would get custody and she didn't fight me about it."

"And you're angry at yourself because you didn't see this before you married her."

The words tumbled out of my mouth before I stop them. I wanted to reach out and grab them and shove them back in but it was far too late. I'd said them out loud.

And all because I knew exactly how he felt. I should have known what David was before I married him. But I didn't and I still hadn't quite come to terms with that.

Jack stared at me for a long time as if he couldn't believe I'd said it out loud either, but then he took a deep breath and nodded. He wasn't angry, thank goodness. I wouldn't have blamed him if he was. It was none of my business.

"Yes. I should have seen it earlier, but I didn't. Now Tyler is paying for my mistake. At least you didn't have kids with your husband."

David took great pride in being a man-child. A baby would have put a crimp in his lifestyle.

"Tyler seems pretty happy. My mom always says that a child knows when they're loved."

"Your mother is a wise woman. I hope she's right."

"She usually is. It's annoying."

Jack didn't have to respond as my phone chirped in my pocket. Quickly checking the display, a picture of Missy had lit up the screen.

"Excuse me, Jack. I need to take this. Help yourself to more pie. Or anything else you want."

I ducked into the pantry to get some privacy but mostly to give Jack some alone time. He wasn't a man that enjoyed revealing anything personal and he wouldn't be happy about doing it today.

"Hey, what's going on?"

"He won't cross over. He says he wants to hunt down his killer."

It only took a moment for me to wrap my mind around who *he* was. Bill Warner. Missy, of course, would have tried to guide him into the light. She was having a rough time lately.

"So he knows who killed him?" I asked excitedly. This was a huge breakthrough although I wasn't sure how we'd tell Jack.

"No, but he wants to figure it out and hunt them down. I tried to talk him out of it but then he got mad and ran. Edward just showed up and he says that Warner is at the movie theater."

"Is that where you're headed?"

"Yes, and you might want to join me."

"Why?"

"Because Daisy and your mother are headed there as well."

I am an optimist. I am an optimist.

"Why?"

"Because Edward was hanging out at the diner with Amelia and Charles when Terrence showed up and told them about the new guy at the movie theater. Daisy overheard and I guess your mom was there. They've decided to help *me* and go talk to him."

"This wedding has gotten out of control."

"Actually, I was thinking your closet ghost is out of control."

"He likes to hang out at the movie theater. That's not a crime. And what about Edward? He's acting like he's not dead. That's out of control."

"Arguing isn't going to get us anywhere. Are you going to meet me there?"

Of course, I was.

Because I was an optimist.

Chapter Thirteen

I HAD SENT Jack away after wrapping up an entire new apple pie for him. If he'd noticed me giving him the bum's rush he didn't say anything. He had a great deal on his plate as well. He wanted to interview Laura Mandrell again, plus go over the evidence one more time. He'd also muttered something about talking to all of the suspects and making sure they didn't leave town. I assumed he was not happy about Sasha's departure this morning but that horse was already out of the barn.

When I arrived at the theater Missy's car was there along with another vehicle I didn't recognize. Perhaps Daisy had traded in her beloved VW bus? I could believe that, but I don't think I'd believe that she'd buy the shiny red convertible parked next to Missy's much more practical sedan. That really only left one person it could belong to.

My mother.

Peggy Hamilton – the original minivan mom – had purchased a sports car for herself. Talk about a midlife crisis. What had my dad bought? A Formula One racecar? Maybe an airplane? Or a rocket ship to the moon? At this point, not much could shock me.

I am an optimist.

The door to the theater was unlocked. Ted the theater guy didn't show up until around dinnertime to start popping the popcorn for the seven o'clock showing but I had to assume that either Daisy, Missy, or my mother had a spare key. Or they'd somehow learned how to pick a lock. Knowing Ravenmist the way I did, it might have simply been unlocked in the first place.

There was no one in the lobby but I could hear voices in the theater. Sure enough, there was Missy, Daisy, and my mother talking – bickering, really – with a nearly transparent Bill Warner.

"Mom, did you buy a convertible?"

Because that was the most important subject at the moment.

Peggy gave me a withering look. "I did."

"It's not very practical."

"That was the point."

Missy wasn't dressed in her Grim Reaper garb, so it looked like Bill Warner was playing hardball about crossing over. He crossed his arms over his chest when he saw me.

"And you aren't going to convince me to go into the light, either. I'm staying right here so I can find out who did this to me and then ruin their career."

"Probably going to prison will do that," my mother observed.

Warner shook his head. "Then I'll make sure they don't get a book deal. Or a movie about their life."

Hollywood sure was different.

"I'm not here to try and get you to cross over," I explained. That was Missy's job. "I'm trying to find out who killed you and Brock Mandrell. What's the last thing you can remember before…you know?"

Bill frowned and gave me a suspicious look. "Why do you even care?"

"My friend Sasha is a suspect and I know she didn't do it. I want to find out who did."

"Sasha didn't do this to me. Laura Mandrell did. I know it."

A collective gasp went up from Missy, Daisy, and my mother. After hearing Sasha talk about Brock's wife, I wasn't as shocked.

"Then you saw her shoot you?"

"No, I was shot in the back. But I know she did it."

What was it about dead people assigning blame even when they hadn't seen their killer?

My mother had been listening to half-baked stories for years from her three children. It didn't appear that she was buying this one at all.

"So you only think she did it?" my mother asked, her hands on her hips. "You don't know for sure, do you?"

Bill's eyes widened at being questioned. "I do so know. I know that she threatened to kill me when she found out that I'd told Brock about her behind the scenes moves. She was furious."

"Behind the scenes moves?" Daisy echoed. "What do you mean?"

He sighed and looked like he wasn't going to answer for a moment. "Laura had a little deal going on in the background. One she didn't want Brock to know anything about because he would have scuttled it the minute he found out. He didn't like competition from his own wife, or from anyone, for that matter."

Missy tapped her toe impatiently. "You still haven't explained what the deal was."

"Right...okay, Laura never got over having to give up her career. So I guess she and Jessica got friendly on the set of the movie and when Jessica was named the director of an indie film that starts shooting in the summer, Laura talked herself into a juicy role. I acted as her agent for the part. We were all supposed to keep it secret from Brock."

"But you didn't do that." What a slime ball.

Bill shrugged. "You gotta go with who has the power and Brock had it. After I told him, he and Laura had a huge fight. Epic. When he showed up dead a few hours later, they didn't want anyone to know because it would look like motive."

My mother was the sweetest Southern belle you'd ever want to meet. Unless she didn't like you. Then...run.

"Well, bless your black heart." My mother was wagging a finger under Bill's transparent nose. "You're a horrible human being, you know that? Have you ever heard of loyalty? Or kindness? What does friendship mean to you?"

"Not much," he replied promptly. "I go with money and power, lady. Which is why I'm not going into that light. I know which way I'm heading. No way. I'm going to stay here and haunt this theater. I'll watch movies and scare teenagers and little kids. It will be a great way to spend my afterlife."

The man had a plan, although I didn't much like the sound of it. Especially the part about scaring little kids. That just sounded mean.

"I might have something to say about that."

A man's voice. It wasn't one of our own and Bill hadn't spoken either. Had I finally gone crazy? Nothing would have surprised me at this moment.

Missy groaned and rolled her eyes. "Samuel, show yourself. This isn't funny."

Samuel? I had a feeling…

Slowly, a man appeared before us, dressed in a gray pin-striped suit. From the forties? Fifties, perhaps? Not much more than that if his hairstyle and shoes were anything to go by.

Missy threw up her hands. "Samuel, are you ready to cross over yet?"

The man, who had a great deal of energy because he didn't look at all like a spirit, shook his head.

"You checked on me just a few months ago. I said no then and I'll say no now. I'm not going."

I nudged my best friend's arm. "I'm beginning to think that your job is far more stressful than my own."

"They're not all like this but some are particularly stubborn."

Samuel turned to Bill. "I heard your plan to haunt this theater. You'll need to find someplace else. I'm the ghost in residence here. This is my home."

Peggy's eyes were round, her gaze darting back and forth between each ghost. Daisy wasn't looking any better and she placed her hand on her chest and heaved a shaky breath.

"Are they going to fight? Can ghosts hurt themselves?"

"No," Missy answered shortly. "They are not going to fight and they can't hurt themselves. They're dead and they can't get any deader. They're also acting like children. Samuel, you don't own this theater, and you can't make Bill move somewhere else. You'll need to find a way to share this space."

"Can so," Samuel shot back. "I've been here for more than sixty years. I've watched some of the greatest films of our time in this theater from the golden age of Hollywood. Garbo. Gable. Harlow. Kelly and Astaire. Real talent. Not the garbage they put out now. It's all car chases and blown-up buildings. Give me *Singin' in the Rain* anytime over that."

Bill's face lit up. Literally. He had a surge of energy, possibly drawing from Samuel. "I love that movie. And what about *Citizen Kane*? Or *The Thin Man* movies? Or anything with Clark Gable. That's why I went to Hollywood. I wanted to be a part of all that."

Somehow Bill had fallen off that path and became a cynic. It was a powerful lesson for me.

Samuel grinned and rubbed his hands together. "I love *The Thin Man* movies. Ted does black and white movies every Wednesday night. What did you say your name was again?"

Bill held out his hand. "Bill. Bill Warner, with the Rogers

and Warner Agency."

"You're an agent."

"I am. I mean…I was. And you?"

Samuel puffed up and smoothed his lapels. "I was a movie critic for the newspaper. I met and interviewed Rita Hayworth. Bogart, too. Nice guy. I could tell you about it. If you want."

"I'd really like to hear about that."

Bill had apparently forgotten his plan of revenge and can I say *thank goodness*? We didn't need a new spirit running around making trouble. We had more than we needed already.

"Let me show you around and I'll tell you the story."

Just like that the two spirits were buddies.

"What just happened here?" my mother asked as the men faded from sight.

Missy shrugged. "They bonded over classic films. Now that they have company, they're never going to cross over."

"We should have invited them to the wedding," Daisy said. "I bet they'd have fun, and they'd get to meet a lot of people."

"Ghosts," I corrected. "You mean they'd get to meet other ghosts."

"Well…I put a sign up in the diner window that everyone in town was invited."

I am an optimist.

It was a wonder I was still sane. In fact, I might not be. They say that the person is the last to know when they've lost it.

Missy had turned pale but my mother was smiling like a Cheshire cat. I had a strange feeling that she had something to do with this.

"You invited…everyone?"

"All the townspeople think that Amelia and Charles are Daisy's cousins. They're a little pale but otherwise they look like you and me," my mother explained. "They shouldn't be ostracized because they're dead."

Missy's brows shot up. "They *should be* crossed over. They shouldn't be dancing around with the living."

"They don't want to cross over," Daisy explained patiently. "They like the in-between."

"Especially if we make it so much fun," I replied sarcastically. The cynic in me was banging at the cage's bars to come out and play. "Please tell me how this is a good idea. If the town finds out they're spirits, we're going to have a problem. A big one."

Groaning, Missy rubbed at her temples. "We already have one, remember? Demons, and evil things, and apocalypse warnings. Oh my."

Daisy and Peggy were wearing matching puzzled expressions.

"I didn't really want Missy to mention all of that but yes, the town has a problem with all of this supernatural energy. Spoiler alert. It's not good."

"I think you need to tell us all about this," my mother said.

Daisy nodded in agreement. "We might be able to help. Four heads are better than two."

That had always been the prevailing wisdom but I bet neither of these women had seen a four-headed demon. I know that I never wanted to.

"Fine, but I'm going to want a turkey dinner to explain it all."

"And pie," Missy added. "Preferably lemon meringue."

Daisy picked up her handbag from one of the theater chairs. "Then let's get to the diner. I want to hear about this."

We walked out of the theater and through the lobby, my mother only pausing to toss a gum wrapper into the trash can near the concession stand. As she stepped forward, she seemed to lose her balance but quickly righted herself by grabbing the candy display, almost sending boxes of gummy bears flying. I jumped to her side but she'd already caught herself.

"Are you okay?" I looked down at her shoes. She was wearing sneakers, not heels. "You need to be careful, Mom."

I was just about to say that she wasn't as young as she used to be when she moved her foot, showing a loose floorboard. That's what she'd tripped on.

"This old floor is starting to come up. They've been talking about fixing it for years now, and they really need to do something about it."

She reached down to put it back in place but then she gasped and froze, her eyes wide. Pointing down to the floor, her hand shook.

"Do you see what I see?"

Not really, because my mother was blocking the hole, but then she moved back and I could clearly see into the small opening under the floor.

A gun. Tucked right under the floorboard.

Jack had never found the murder weapon and they'd done a thorough sweep of the theater, but I highly doubted they'd pulled up floorboards. If it was even there when they'd looked. Anyone could have come back here and hidden it at any time. As I'd seen when I arrived, this place wasn't exactly Fort Knox in security.

"I do see it, Mom. We need to take that to Jack."

Would it be too much to ask for there to be fingerprints?

Chapter Fourteen

JACK LIVED IN the condo development on the edge of town. It wasn't my kind of place with its identical beige facades. Every house had one tree, one mailbox, and a short box shrub near the front door. Sure, some families had gone all out and planted flowers or had a potted plant on the tiny front porch, but as I drove down his street it was difficult to tell one home from another.

His place didn't have any flowers or plants or even their name on the mailbox. Just the street number identified his home. That and the police SUV in the driveway. That was a dead giveaway.

When I'd stopped by the sheriff's station his assistant had said that Jack had stopped at home for a little while because Tyler wasn't feeling well. I hadn't wanted to hand over the gun to just anybody, so now I was parking in front of Jack's condo and wondering about the wisdom of this decision. Maybe I should have just given it to one of the deputies after all.

It was funny that I didn't think anything about having Jack around at the inn eating my food and drinking my coffee. It didn't seem strange, but my being here at his house? That seemed far too personal. Like I was treading on sacred ground. We might be friends but this might be a bridge too far for him.

Oh well. He'd get over it eventually. He really needed to relax more and enjoy life.

Pressing the doorbell, I waited on the front porch, checking out his neighbors who appeared to be mostly not at home. Since it was the middle of the afternoon, I assumed they were at work. A dog barked in the distance and a package delivery truck trundled down the road slowly, but all in all this was one quiet street.

The door swung open and Tyler stood there, a welcome grin on his face. "Hey, Tedi. Come on in. I didn't know you were coming over."

"Neither did I until a few minutes ago," I confessed. "I stopped at the station but they said your dad was here. I heard you were sick. I hope you're feeling better."

"It's just a stupid cold. I was coughing and one of my teachers is a germaphobe. She made me see the school nurse who called my dad."

"Is it Mrs. Lasky, by any chance?"

"How did you know?"

"Nothing ever changes. She used to clean the desks and doorknobs in between classes with antibacterial wipes. We learned to hold in our sneezes."

Unless, of course, we wanted to go home. Then we'd just pretend to sneeze or cough a few times and we'd be exiled. Sadly, the school nurse eventually caught on to what we were doing and just sent us to the library until our next class. Nothing good lasts forever.

"Do you need to talk to Dad? I'll go get him. He said he was going to take a quick nap."

Before I could stop him, Tyler bolted from the room and down a hallway. Great, now I was going to be blamed for interrupting Jack's nap. I had a feeling he didn't do this often too, but he'd been burning the candle at both ends since Brock Mandrell's death. The press was merciless on the "small town sheriff" and whether he could solve the crime without some big city help.

Since I was left standing in Jack's living room, I took the opportunity to do some snooping, checking for photos on the wall and looking for anything that might tell me more about the person that I was becoming friends with.

Nothing. Nada. Zip-o-rama.

Beige. Jack must love the color beige because most of what I saw around me was that bland shade. The carpet, the kitchen tile, the walls, the furniture.

Beige. It didn't tell me much about him. It was as if the sheriff was in the witness protection program.

There were also no photos on the walls or any other surface. No books or newspapers on the coffee table. No funny mugs on the kitchen counter. There was a plate peeking out of the sink but it was…plain white. It made a nice change from beige.

I heard a familiar growl and then the sound of stomping feet on the beige wall to wall carpeting before Jack appeared in the living room, blinking sleepily and running his fingers through his hair.

"Hey, Jack. Sorry to interrupt your beauty sleep."

I shouldn't have sounded sarcastic but if I didn't, I would have reached out and smoothed down his hair, standing on end from his pillow. What was it about this man that made me want to take care of him?

"What are you doing here, Tedi?"

So much for being happy to see me. But I knew how to turn that frown upside down.

"You'd think you'd be nicer to me when I've brought you a present."

"A present?"

His eyes were narrowed in suspicion and considering our past relationship I didn't blame him one bit.

"We were at the theater—"

"Why?"

His one-word question was shot back at rapid fire speed. However, it was a question I couldn't answer. Not honestly. I couldn't tell him that Missy and I were looking for a renegade soul.

"I needed a few photos for my website. I'm adding a local attraction page."

Actually, I wasn't but I guess I was now. Knowing Jack, he'd check to make sure I was telling the truth.

"And you came here to tell me about it?"

Sighing, I leaned a hip against the back of the beige couch. "You really should get a better attitude when visitors come to call. As you know, I'm trying to be more optimistic. You should try it."

"How's it going for you?"

He had no idea. The struggle is real.

"Peachy, thank you for asking. Now back to my present." I held up the sweater wrapped around the gun. "We didn't touch it with our hands. We used Missy's sweater. I hope we didn't mess up any prints."

"Prints?"

I had his attention. Finally. He'd straightened up and looked far more awake than he had only a couple of minutes ago.

"There was this loose floorboard and my mother tripped," I explained. "Anyway, to make a long story short...there was a gun under the loose floorboard. We thought it might be your murder weapon."

That's when I pushed back part of the wool sweater, showing off the heavy firearm within. Jack's eyes widened and then he started to smile.

"Great day in the morning. You just may have found it, Tedi."

"Actually, it was my mom. She's the one that tripped."

I couldn't take all the credit.

"But I was the one that told them not to touch it. I just have this feeling it's what you've been looking for."

Okay, I took *some* credit.

Jack looked down at the gun and then back up at me.

"You didn't give this to the deputy on duty?"

"I wouldn't give it to anyone but you."

Taking the parcel from me, he reached for his car keys on the end table. "I'm going to take this to the county lab right now. We'll see if they can pull any prints or DNA from it. This just might crack the case."

"You're welcome."

"Thank you, Tedi."

I waved away his thanks. "Not necessary. I'm happy to help. Just being a good citizen."

"A nosy citizen, but this time it paid off."

"You're not going to find Sasha's prints on it."

He slipped into his shoes. "Unlike you, I don't have an opinion about what they might find. It doesn't matter to me who the killer is. I just want to find them and put them behind bars."

"She didn't do it."

"Then you have nothing to worry about."

That was about as far from the truth as it could be.

AFTER DROPPING OFF the gun to Jack, I went back to the inn determined to sit down and finish the paperwork that had been collecting on my desk. I was barely in the front door, however, when my manager accosted me, dragging me toward the sitting room.

When I looked into the half-open doorway, Laura Mandrell and Darrell Kennedy were sitting on the Queen Anne style couch giving an interview to Caroline Hayes, known for her Barbara Walters' style celebrity interviews. Based on Caroline's previous interviews I imagined that Laura and Darrell would be in tears before long.

Frankly, I was annoyed.

I didn't like it when I didn't know what was going on in my own inn. I also didn't like it that Laura and Darrell had invited in the press and made themselves at home in my sitting room without so much as a heads up to me. Or my staff.

I heard a soft sob and then Laura pulled out a handkerchief, dabbing at her eyes. She was perfectly made up, looking lovely in a pale green dress with matching heels. Darrell looked...well...like Darrell usually did. A bit rumpled. I think he was going for eccentric.

"They won't let us leave," Darrell complained in a loud voice. "They're keeping us hostage here. Is the sheriff planning to keep us forever? What if he never finds who did this?"

Uh oh. Kennedy had just made a shot over the bow. Jack would not be pleased. It hadn't been that long and they weren't hostages. Technically, they could leave whenever they wanted to. Jack had asked them not to go while he was investigating the murders.

Laura nodded, sniffling delicately into her hanky. "If the sheriff can't find the killer then he needs to admit it and ask for help. Call in the state police or the FBI. Get private investigators working on it. I'll pay for it. I think he just needs to admit that he's failed."

Oh…Oh no. She didn't. Oh, she did. She used the f-word. *Fail.* At the press conference she'd been Jack's biggest fan, but now she'd turned on him. This was going to be so bad. There wasn't enough apple pie and ice cream in the whole county to keep Jack calm.

"Why do you think he won't let you leave?" Caroline asked with just the right amount of concern in her voice.

"Because he's trying to put the blame on us," Laura proclaimed, her chin lifted defiantly.

Darrell nodded in agreement. "That's right. If he can't find the real killer then we'll do as scapegoats. We're being railroaded."

Cue the dramatic sobbing from Laura. Darrell put his arm around her in comfort, saying something I couldn't hear in her ear.

For heaven's sake. They were doing a play, not giving in interview. It was all an act for the cameras.

And the cameras – and Caroline Hayes – were eating it all up. She had two victims and a bad guy – one Sheriff Jack Garrett. I had a terrible feeling that Jack's past was going to be aired out for all to see and judge. For a private person such as himself this was going to be a nightmare.

I wasn't sure what I should do. Kick them out? Stride into the interview and tell them all off?

I didn't have a chance to make a decision because Missy had

snuck up behind me and was tugging on my arm.

"What are you doing?" she whispered.

"Listening in to this interview. Laura and Darrell are throwing Jack under the bus. They say he's failed."

Missy's jaw went slack and I heard her suck in her breath. "The sheriff isn't going to take too kindly to that."

"That is the understatement of the year. He's going to flip his lid. I wouldn't be surprised if he runs them all in for disturbing the peace."

"They're not being loud."

"But I'm not feeling tranquil, are you? They've definitely disturbed my peace."

She held up a piece of paper. "I'm not going to help that. I have the names of all the people that have moved to Ravenmist in the last year. We need to go through them."

Right. That pesky demon situation.

"Then let's get to it and figure out who brought an apocalypse to Ravenmist."

Chapter Fifteen

THERE WERE SIX people on the list. Six. That wasn't much to choose from.

I'd made Missy and I a pot of tea and we'd retreated to my apartment to discuss the pros and cons of each person. I'd also swiped a pound cake from the kitchen on our way because a girl needs sustenance. How else was I going to keep my strength up?

Edward and Terrence were at my tiny kitchen table hovering over my old laptop, editing their latest footage, earphones on. Apparently, the documentary was going well. When they won their Oscar, I could say I knew them when.

"What are you two doing?" Edward asked as Missy and I dug into matching slabs of cake. Delicious. I'd needed a zap of sugar.

We hadn't specifically told the ghosts about the demon or any of Madame Harriet's predictions about them being enslaved to evil. If she wasn't correct, we didn't want to cause a panic. On the other hand, forewarned is forearmed. I was open to telling them about it but Missy silently shook her head. Clearly, she thought it was a bad idea. So noted. Lips buttoned.

"It's a to-do list for our high school reunion," she replied.

"I'm one of the co-chairs."

It wasn't a bad cover story. It was never too early to start planning.

Edward scowled and groaned. "A reunion? Why would you do that?"

"Because we actually like people. Do you want to help?"

We already knew their answer and it was a big, fat no. They were completely obsessed with this documentary idea. Missy and I loved it too, as it kept them busy and out of our hair. Win-win.

"We're pretty busy," Terrence said. "Maybe another time?"

They didn't even wait for our answer, putting their earphones back on and completely ignoring Missy and myself.

Excellent.

I tapped the list with my pencil. "I think we can rule out Jack and Tyler from the get-go. He hates the idea of anything supernatural and makes fun of it."

Missy frowned. "I don't like the idea of ruling anyone out right away. I think we need to keep an open mind."

"An open mind? About Jack? Do you honestly think he's a demon?"

Be real.

"You're always saying what a pain he is..."

That was true.

"Okay, that's a pro for Jack as a demon. But his complete disbelief in ghosts has to be a con."

"Maybe he doesn't really know ghosts exist?" Missy asked reasonably. "I didn't know demons were real so it's possible."

"Madame Harriet said that demons can rule over spirits, so I would imagine he would know."

"If she was correct in the first place. She's only telling us what has been passed down for generations. They don't write the rules in a book, unfortunately."

"If there was a book like that, I'd buy it."

"We all would. Now I think Jack being young, healthy, and powerful would be a pro. He could house a heck of a lot of energy inside of him."

"But he's not a very nice person. That's got to be a con. Somehow, I imagine a good demon fighting evil for the universe as a little more personable. A people-demon, so to speak."

Missy nodded and then quirked an eyebrow. "Then what about Tyler?"

"Can Tyler be a demon if Jack isn't?"

Sighing, she shook her head. "Not unless he's adopted and he looks just like his dad. So we're saying that if Jack is a demon then Tyler is one, too. That's a bunch of energy with two demons. We need to keep them on the list."

I still wasn't convinced.

"If he's a good demon, then why bring all that energy here to Ravenmist and start a war? Why didn't he stay in Chicago with all the other demons and have his energy in the power-soup that is a big city? Then no one would be coming after him specifically."

"You're right, it doesn't make any sense," Missy conceded. "But then it doesn't make any sense at all why a good demon would come to our town and make it a target for evil. I hope whomever it turns out to be has a darn good reason for doing it."

I couldn't think of one good reason, but then I wasn't a demon – good or evil or something in-between. Were there any undecided demons who just couldn't commit to a side? They wanted to be good but the cookies on the evil side were simply delicious so they were torn.

"How about Ike Hillborn? He's a strange one. Doesn't talk to many people. Keeps to himself."

"That doesn't mean he's a demon."

"I don't know about that," I shot back. "Whenever you hear about a murderer on the news the people around them always say something like *he was a loner* or *he was so quiet.*"

"Maybe demons don't have a lot to say. Maybe they're introverts. Ike Hillborn comes into the bookstore every week and he's always nice and polite. Pays in cash and never tries to return anything."

"That nails it for me then. I bet demons don't have credit cards."

Missy giggled and almost choked on her pound cake. "Can you imagine it? The First National Bank of Demons. Free checking and low interest home loans. I wonder if they have novelty checks like with cartoon characters or cute animals?"

"If I were a demon I'd have Scooby-Doo checks."

"You *have* Scooby-Doo checks."

Exactly. If I were a demon, I'd still want fun checks. Not that I used them much anymore. I couldn't remember the last time I'd even written a check. Maybe…last year? I think I'd written one to my sister when we'd all gone in together on a gift for my mother.

"Okay, we need to keep moving. Delia and Richard Carmody. I could see it. They could be demons."

"Tedi," Missy scolded, her brows pinched together. "Delia and Richard Carmody have to be about a hundred years old. I don't think they're up for an epic fight with evil. They came to town to be closer to their grandkids."

"They could be pretending to be old. You know…to fool us all. They might be great warriors."

"I heard Delia saying that Richard just had a hip replaced. I don't think he's a great warrior."

"That only leaves one name on the list. Helena Miller." I searched my memory but couldn't place her. "It doesn't ring any bells."

Missy frowned and rubbed her chin. "It doesn't ring any bells with me either, but she moved here one year ago almost to the day. She lives in the same condo development as Jack."

"Then we know what we have to do."

Find out everything we could about Helena Miller. If she was the demon, we'd find out. Somehow.

Not that I had any clue what the plan would be if she *was* a demon. We'd figure that out later.

RAVENMIST'S SMALL SIZE – and our resourcefulness – made it easy to find out a few details about Helena Miller.

Right. You guessed it. Missy and I asked Daisy the next morning at the diner.

But to get there we had to wade through a sea of protestors picketing the sheriff's office. They all had signs that proclaimed Laura and Darrell's innocence or demands to free them. Despite the fact that Jack wasn't holding them against their will.

I was shocked to see them there as Jack didn't take much to rabble-rousers in his town, but someone must have pulled him aside and whispered in his ear because the mob of a few dozen people weren't being swept off the sidewalk. He was allowing them their First Amendment rights, which was a good thing because I'd noticed that the press had also gotten wind of this mini-demonstration and they were lying in wait across the street, salivating as they waited for the small town sheriff to do something stupid and try to break up the crowd. They'd have video of that splashed all over the world in ten seconds flat, making Ravenmist and Jack look like backwater idiots.

I was also pretty darn sure that Laura and Darrell had known exactly what they were doing giving that interview yesterday. It was already all over the internet and now the reporters were waiting for the powder keg that was our venerable town to blow sky high. The wife and the director were getting some serious mileage in the press out of this situation. Personally, I'm not sure that I'd want to remind people that I was under suspicion of murder, but obviously they'd decided it was a good idea.

What was the saying? Any publicity is good publicity? It was something like that.

By the time we slid into a booth inside the Grateful Raven I had worked up an appetite. It was clearly a day for waffles. Missy ordered a ham and cheese omelet. We both ordered coffee, and lots of it.

Halfway through the meal, Daisy came to join us. As usual she was a fountain of information about everyone and everything going on in Ravenmist. What she didn't know wasn't worth learning.

"She works at the cosmetic counter at Simpson's department store," Daisy told us. "Single but looking. She moved here because she was tired of the rat race in Indianapolis."

Likely story. It sounded just like something that a demon might make up.

"There's a rat race in Indianapolis?" I scoffed. "And she just happened to pick Ravenmist out of a hat? She couldn't have chosen us by throwing a dart at a map because we're too small to even be on most maps. Something is fishy with that story."

Daisy held up her hands in surrender. "I'm just telling you what she's said. And I'm sure there is a rat race in Indianapolis. Don't they have a big race there every year?"

Yes, but that was a different kind of race.

We also learned that Helena was in her mid-forties, liked cats, and baking cakes. She also liked to travel and she went on a big trip once a year with a few friends.

"She comes in a few times a week for dinner," Daisy said.

"She said that sometimes she doesn't want to cook dinner for one. You've seen her too, Tedi. She has pale blonde hair that she always wears up. She's tall, too."

I shrugged. "I got nothing. I don't remember her."

Hey, I meet a lot of people every day. I can't remember them all.

"You'd remember her if you saw her. It's weird that you haven't crossed paths before now. She's always out and about around town."

It was strange, which only served to make me more suspicious.

I made my decision then and there.

"I think I need a makeover," I stated, slapping the table for emphasis. A few heads whipped around but when they saw it was me they didn't think anything of it, simply going back to their food.

Missy wrinkled her nose and sighed. "I mean...I guess we all could...but you're being too hard on yourself, Tedi. Okay, you could update your look a little bit. You've worn the same lipstick since high school...but a makeover might be a little overboard."

With friends like these, who needs demons?

I held up my pointer finger. "First of all, that lipstick looks great on me. It's the perfect nude shade for my complexion."

I held up two fingers. "Secondly, I wasn't talking about actually needing a real makeover. That's just what I'm going to say to Helena when you and I go to Simpson's department store."

Missy shook her head, her eyes round. "That's not a good

idea. If she's really a demon we should probably keep our distance."

"Then what's all this been about?" I argued. "Why bother to find out possible demons if we have to stay away?"

"Because I'm working on a way to identify a demon," Missy replied. "At least my grandmother is. She's checking every book we've got to see if there's something we can do to unmask our demon friend. Then – and only then – we can get close and find out."

"You could use a new moisturizer," Daisy said helpfully. "After thirty…"

Daisy was spending far too much time with my mother. She was also harping on my using moisturizer every day and not wearing too much blush.

"See? I need a new moisturizer." I shoved the last bite of waffle in my mouth. "You don't have to go if you don't want to."

"Of course, I'll go," Missy sighed. "You shouldn't approach any demon – even a good one – all by yourself. Assuming that she's the demon. She might not be."

"I'll just meet her, get a new moisturizer, and go home. No big deal. I just want to see her."

"You can't tell if she's a demon just by looking at her," Missy warned. "It doesn't work that way."

I think I could tell. Surely I'd have some sort of gut feeling. Right?

"Then I'll get a new moisturizer. Geez, have another cup of

coffee. You're cranky when you don't have enough caffeine."

Daisy clasped her hands together and gave me a big smile. "What about you, Tedi? Would you like more coffee?"

I always want more coffee. Silly question.

"I wouldn't mind a warmup, thank you."

Daisy retrieved a full carafe and refilled our mugs before sitting back down. "Tedi, I need a favor."

So the coffee had merely been a bribe. Well played, Daisy. Well played.

"How can I help?"

"This wedding has gotten a trifle out of hand." She waved her arm theatrically. "The guest list is larger than we originally planned–"

"Wait...who all is coming?"

Last I'd heard she'd invited the entire town but had they all RSVP'd? Didn't anyone in this town have something to do on Saturday?

Daisy tapped her chin. "Let's see...um...just about every-one."

"Everyone?" I echoed, fear stabbing my heart. What had she done? "What do you mean by *everyone*, Daisy?"

"Pretty much everyone that has come in this week said they were going to come."

I felt faint.

"I'm not a math whiz, Daisy, but that sounds like a bunch of people."

She nodded. "It might be a few hundred."

A few hundred. People.

"You invited a few hundred people to watch two ghosts exchange vows?" I whispered, leaning closer to we wouldn't be overheard. "What if they notice that they're not breathing, Daisy? What will we do then?"

"No one will notice. They didn't at the Valentine Ball, and if anything, the spirits have more energy now than they did then."

True, but I still believed that we got lucky.

"Everyone will be looking at the happy couple. Everyone will be staring at them. I'm not sure they can pass that kind of inspection. Does Amelia even have a wedding dress?"

Daisy's face lit up. "She does. I bought both their outfits online. Very dressy and old-fashioned. She'll be a lovely bride and Charles a handsome groom."

"A really dead one, though. We can't let people figure this out. What if someone tries to give them a hug? They'll get zapped by all of that power."

"Maybe we can tell people that Amelia and Charles aren't the huggy type," Missy suggested. "Or that they're both coming down with a cold. No one wants the crud."

"There's always one in every crowd that doesn't listen," I lamented. "My Aunt Gertrude doesn't care that I value personal space and bodily autonomy. She just goes in for the hug whether I like it or not."

Another thought occurred to me.

"Did you tell people no gifts? Because now that this wedding is an event people might bring gifts. What do two people who have been dead for a hundred years really need?"

"Edward and Terrence really like your old laptop," Missy said with a chuckle. "And Charles loves technology. We could get him a cell phone."

"Who is he going to call?"

"He likes to play with the apps. No one uses their phone to actually talk to people anymore."

And that's why we were facing an apocalypse.

"That reminds me," Daisy said. "Edward and Terrence are going to video the wedding. They want to add it to their documentary."

Why not? The world didn't make much sense anymore. They thought I was the crazy one. Ha!

"So can we have the wedding at the inn?" Daisy asked, giving me the puppy dog eyes. "I'll take care of everything. The food, the decorations, the music. I just need a room large enough to hold all of the people."

I was born at night but it wasn't last night, folks.

"You've already told them that it's at the inn, haven't you?"

Daisy had the decency to blush. "Well...I told them that it was the likely venue. Missy suggested it."

I was outnumbered, outvoted, and generally outmaneuvered. Guests were going to start showing up at my inn at noon tomorrow expecting a wedding.

"What time will you be showing up tomorrow to get ready?"

It's always better to give in gracefully than to fight a war that no one is interested in.

Both Daisy and Missy beamed at my capitulation. "I'd like to start tonight if that's okay."

That would be fine. I was now the ghost-hostess with the mostest.

One spirited wedding coming up.

Chapter Sixteen

DAISY BAILED ON my mission to find out more about Helena Miller but Missy dutifully trudged at my side to Simpson's department store. The strong scent of perfume had us following our noses to the cosmetic department where Helena was standing behind the counter arranging samples of hand cream.

"Okay, so the story is that I need a new moisturizer. Got it?"

Missy sighed and shook her head. "We shouldn't be doing this. It's a terrible idea."

"If she's a good demon, she's not going to hurt us and if she's not a demon then I'll have a new moisturizer."

"What if she's something else?"

"I'm not following you."

"We've recently learned that demons exist. We know that ghosts and reapers exist. Perhaps there are other beings that we don't know about."

I didn't like the thought of that at all.

"What are the chances? Has to be infinitesimal. Let's do this."

"Okay, but don't act weird."

"Define weird."

"Don't stare or ask a bunch of questions. Just…act normal."

The normal train had long ago left the station.

"Sure, I can do that."

Probably not.

As we approached the circular glass counter, Helena's gaze zeroed in on us and her smile widened. Obviously she recognized a potential customer.

"Ladies, what can I do for you today?"

I opened my mouth to tell her that I needed moisturizer but Missy was quicker off the block. That wily minx had it in for me.

"My friend needs a complete makeover."

Helena must have heard angels sing – along with several dollar signs. Her entire visage lit up and she clapped her hands together like an enthusiastic seal.

"I'll get you for this," I whispered to Missy, giving her an elbow in the ribs. "When you least expect it…expect it."

I had a long memory.

An hour later my face wasn't recognizable and my wallet was quite a bit lighter than when I'd entered the store. Seriously, when I looked into the hand mirror that Helena held up a stranger was looking back.

I'm no slouch when it comes to doing my own makeup. I know how to enhance my eyes and cover my too-red cheeks, but I was usually quite conservative when it came to slapping some war paint on my face. My mother had always told me *less is more* and I'd followed her advice even in my rebellious teenage years. Okay, there was that purple eyeshadow incident but we don't speak about it now.

Helena, however, had no such inhibitions and she'd happily applied layer upon layer of makeup to my skin until I was gone and some other woman sat in my place. Who was she? Did she like pie?

I'd apparently been *contoured.* At least that's how Helena described it. This was the process of applying darker makeup to the hollows and shadows of my face and lighter to the high points. It was very *in* and *trendy* and *now* we were told. Everyone was doing it. I didn't bring up that I personally didn't know anyone who was doing it because I assumed that I would be told that I didn't know the right, *cool* people.

Let me first say that I've never aspired to be trendy in any way, shape, or form. It's simply not in my DNA. I'd always been a little out of step with fashion and the cool crowds and I was fine with it. I'm used to my own nerdiness. I kind of like it, in fact. So this face…

I'll say this. I am an optimist.

My mother also brought me up to be kind and polite and when I didn't have anything nice to say I should keep my trap shut. However, Helena wasn't down with this because she kept asking me my opinion and then ignoring it. When she asked if I liked a smoky eye, I said no. She did one anyway because I apparently have the perfect shaped eye for that.

I didn't know that. Did you?

I'd also purchased a contouring kit – out of sheer polite-ness – because Helena said that my cheekbones were hiding in my round face. I had to admit that my cheekbones had never looked higher in my entire life. My face looked model-slim. Unfortunately, the rest of me didn't match. I was still Tedi Hamilton from the neck down. Average height. Average weight. Average cheekbones. Thanks, Mom and Dad for the genes.

And for all that I'd been through in the last hour, I wasn't any closer to figuring out if Helena was the demon or not. I'd tried talking about how I was the head of the paranormal society but it turns out that Helena only wanted to talk about the products she was troweling on my face. She was in full sales mode. Heck, even Missy bought some moisturizer.

"You look different," Missy said as we exited the store, both of us carrying bags. Mine was larger than hers, of course, but revenge is a dish best served cold. At least I'd been told that.

"I don't even recognize myself."

"Will you admit that this was a waste of time *now?*"

Sighing in defeat, I nodded. "It was. I guess I just thought I would know when someone was a demon."

"It doesn't work like that. They're like humans except for their souls. I'm a reaper and I can't read souls that deeply."

A fantastic thought occurred to me. "What about your un-cle? He's the mac daddy of reapers. Couldn't he?"

She shook her head. "I asked him and he said no. Demons have a soul and we can feel it but we can't tell if it's human or not. When they die their souls move on just like a regular human. It's only their energy that stays here and generally moves into their offspring. Unless it's stolen."

"How do they steal it?"

"My uncle said it's some sort of ritual done right at death. They can suck the power into themselves. He's trying to get more specific information about it. This isn't something we've had to deal with before so we don't have all the details. And we could be completely wrong. Like Madame Harriet, all we have to go on are the stories that have been handed down from generation to generation. Demons are a secret lot."

"We'll figure this out. We'll find the demon."

"You sound so sure," Missy said with a laugh. "What makes you so confident? I'd like to share in it."

"I am an optimist."

And it wasn't easy.

IT WAS HARD to believe that only an hour ago it had been complete and utter chaos at the inn. It was the day of the wedding and the weather had happily cooperated. The sun shone and the temperature hovered at a mild seventy-two degrees without a raindrop in sight. That meant Daisy could set up most of the reception tables outside while the formal ceremony would take place in my lobby.

Once again, this time at Daisy's behest, men with strong backs had been called into service to clear the lobby of furniture and set up rows of chairs. Somewhere she'd found a wooden arch and she'd covered it with trailing flowers and vines. It really was lovely. She'd gone all out for her spirited houseguests, saying that they deserved it after loving each other for over one hundred years.

Even a recovering cynic such as myself could appreciate the beauty of the day and what Charles and Amelia were about to vow to one another.

I don't know how Daisy managed it but somehow through sheer strength of will she'd brought this occasion together. The tables were covered with snow white tablecloths, the china and silverware – courtesy of me – gleamed in the sunlight. There were flowers everywhere, an explosion of color that set a happy tone for the nuptials.

"Everything is beautiful," Missy breathed when she walked in arm and arm with her boyfriend Dylan. He looked dapper in a blue suit and my best friend was dressed in a floaty floral print that made her look even more like a princess than she normally did. "Daisy really outdid herself today."

"She certainly did. If I ever get married again, I think I'll let her organize my wedding."

Missy nudged Dylan with her elbow. "Tedi is trying to be more optimistic and less cynical."

He looked like he wanted to laugh, his lips twitching, but he had the good manners not to.

"That's...wonderful, Tedi. Have you been checking your blood pressure by any chance?"

"No, but I'm sure it's higher. Thank you for asking."

We'd all grown up together in this little town and Dylan knew me well.

"Holding in your emotions isn't good for you," he said. "It's great to be optimistic but you need to find a way to let off some steam if you need to."

"I've been thinking about learning to throw knives like they do in the circus."

"Or you could crochet," Missy suggested. "That's nice, too."

She didn't even want me knitting. Needles and all. Crochet hooks were less deadly.

"Isn't that your mom, Tedi?" Dylan asked, nodding toward the left side of the lobby. "Looks like she's with Irwin Simpson."

Irwin Simpson was of the Simpson family that owned the local department store where I'd received my makeover yesterday. Speaking of that debacle, I'd washed my face twice when I got home and tucked that contouring kit in the back of a vanity drawer. I'd decided to keep the old me. She might not have great cheekbones but she had a decent sense of humor. The fact was I wasn't nearly skilled enough to manage all that makeup. I'd stick to the basics.

"Go say hi to your mom." Missy gently pushed me in that direction. "We'll go sit down and save you a seat."

My mother had always had a keen sense of fashion and today was no exception. Dressed in a fuchsia suit with an ecru blouse underneath she looked chic and put together. In fact, my mom could probably carry off that contouring stuff from yesterday.

She had great cheekbones. Too bad she didn't pass them down.

"Hey, Mom. Good to see you. You look fantastic."

We hugged and she examined me from head to toe like I was a teenager going out on a date. Some things never changed.

"You look good, too. I like that dress on you."

I can clean up nice when I put in some effort. Today I was wearing a blue sleeveless dress with a scalloped hem line and matching pumps. I'd even tried to tame my red curls and piled them high on top of my head, fastened with a gold barrette.

"Honey, this is my escort Irwin Simpson. Have you two met before?"

We had at some town function but I couldn't remember which it was. He seemed like a good guy, always smiling and helpful. In fact, he kind of reminded me of my dad.

"Nice to see you again, Mr. Simpson." I shook his head. "I heard rumors that you might run for mayor."

His smile widened and he chuckled, his cheeks turning pink. "Those rumors are true. I think Ravenmist needs a shot of new ideas. And please, Tedi, call me Irwin. My dad is Mr. Simpson."

Ravenmist hadn't had new ideas in about two hundred years but good luck to Irwin. A few new thoughts probably wouldn't hurt the town. As long as he didn't want to build high-rises then he'd be fine.

Music began and people began to find their seats. "Shall we sit down?"

My mother shook her head. "You two go ahead. I'm going to take my place under the arch."

Say...what?

"Um...huh? What do you mean, Mom?"

My mother puffed up, a grin on her face. "I'm going to perform the ceremony."

For a moment I thought my mother said that she was going to perform the ceremony.

"I don't think that's legal, Mom."

Not that a wedding between two ghosts was probably legal anyway. But it was the principle of the whole thing.

"I can perform a wedding ceremony. I have a license now. Online. The website said I could perform weddings for fun and profit."

"Online?"

"It took about ten minutes and cost me nineteen-ninety-nine plus tax and shipping."

"Shipping?"

"They're going to ship me a lovely certificate suitable for framing. Until then, I was able to print one up in case anyone asked about my credentials."

Who on earth was going to do that? The bride and groom were deceased.

Irwin cleared his throat. "I see someone I know. If you ladies will excuse me..."

We would and we did. Irwin shot across the room to talk to the current mayor of Ravenmist, leaving me and mom on our own.

"You know that you didn't need to actually get a license to

perform this marriage, right? You know that Amelia and Charles aren't alive?"

"They still deserve a legal wedding, Tedi." My mom sounded annoyed with me, which wasn't that unusual. "They've been in love for more than a hundred years."

I was well aware and yes, I was impressed. But they still didn't need a legal ceremony unless they planned to start living their lives again.

Oh my stars, is that what they were planning? It made finding the good demon and getting them out of Ravenmist even more important than ever. This entire situation was getting completely out of hand. When you can't tell the dead from the living, you have a problem.

"You need to take your seat, Tedi. It's almost time. I have a wedding to perform. My first of hopefully many. When you get married again, I can do yours."

I didn't know what to say so I took my mother's advice to find a seat. There were two chairs empty next to Missy and Dylan so I slid into one and took a deep breath. I was possibly the most nervous person here. More even than the bride and groom. I was terrified someone was going to notice that Amelia and Charles weren't quite alive. Talk about a can of worms…

The music grew louder and I turned to look down the aisle where Amelia was standing, holding a huge bouquet of flowers and smiling happily. After more than a century together, she and Charles were going to tie the knot.

Now that, folks, is optimism.

Chapter Seventeen

THE CEREMONY WAS beautiful and touching. The love that Charles and Amelia had for one another was lovely and I might have teared up slightly. Mom did a great job performing the ceremony and was even able to make the guests laugh a little. I couldn't help but think that Dad would be really proud of her, but then I reminded myself that he was in Miami with his new girlfriend. They were divorced – or soon would be – and they had both clearly moved on.

As for anyone noticing that the bride and groom weren't alive, not one person seemed to notice. There were oohs and ahhs when Amelia walked down the aisle in her lacy dress and veil but if anyone noticed that she wasn't breathing, they weren't saying it out loud.

The state of denial is a funny thing.

After the vows, the guests were herded out to the patio for the reception. Daisy hadn't had time to get a band so I'd allowed her to play music over my outside speakers. There was a buffet to the left and at the end was a simple tiered wedding cake that Daisy had been working on for days. Late last night, my pastry chef had given her a hand with the decorating so she could get at least a few hours of sleep.

I found a seat next to Missy and Dylan at a table far away from the flurry of the buffet. We'd all filled our plates and I was looking forward to digging in to some of Daisy's famous pot roast. Missy spied someone across the room and waved her hand to get their attention.

"Sheriff, there's an empty chair here."

I hadn't seen Jack since the protestors had shown up and I was kind of glad about that. He couldn't be in a great mood, and when he was like that it was always wise to give him a wide berth. To my surprise, however, he looked normal. Not happy or anything, but not angry either. Just in between.

He hesitated before sitting next to me. "Are you sure this seat isn't taken? What about your mom, Tedi?"

I nodded to where my mother was holding court with Irwin Simpson by her side. She was the belle of the ball.

"She's at another table. You can sit here."

Missy looked inordinately pleased that the sheriff and I were sitting together at this event. The town matchmaking continued, albeit less obviously. For all I knew, all of Ravenmist had made sure that no one sat next to me but Jack.

We ate in silence for a few minutes but shutting up wasn't my natural state. I had questions, people. I wanted answers.

"I didn't expect to see you here today."

Because he was even more cynical than I was.

"Daisy invited me and she sounded like she'd be upset if I

didn't at least show my face. It was a nice ceremony. I didn't know your mom could perform marriages."

"I didn't, either. It's a new development. She got it online."

Chuckling, Jack took a drink of his iced tea. "I guess what they say is true. There really isn't anything you can't get on the internet."

"Where's Tyler?"

"With one of his friends. When I mentioned coming to a wedding, he didn't seem all that excited so I decided to give him a break."

"That was nice of you." I took a nibble of my dinner roll. "Have you heard from the lab about the gun?"

"No, but I should very soon." He patted his phone in his pocket. "I'm keeping it close just in case and only turned it on silent for the ceremony. Thank you again for bringing it to me."

"You should thank my mom for being a klutz. She's the one that tripped on the floorboard."

"I'll do that today. I am grateful. I don't have much to go on right now." His lips twisted. "The governor called me today and tried to get me to accept the help of the state police."

I had a feeling the offer hadn't gone over well with Jack.

"What did you say?"

"I told him no and that I didn't vote for him."

I almost spit out my tea. "You could warn a girl not to take a drink before you say something like that. You didn't really, though? You didn't really say that?"

"I did," he replied grimly. "And I'm not sorry. I don't need a bunch of other cops coming in here acting like we don't know what we're doing. It's all under control. There isn't anything that they could do that I haven't already done. They'd be in the same exact boat that I am."

"But they could take the blame."

The words flew out of my mouth before I could stop them. Jack wasn't the type who worried about blame. Or bad press.

"I'm a grown man, Tedi. If I can't solve these murders then I deserve the blame."

"I know you will."

"I know I will, too." He popped a piece of roast chicken into his mouth. "So how's the optimism going? Are you a convert?"

"It's not easy," I admitted. "But I think it's worth it. You know, Jack, it wouldn't kill you to be a little more optimistic. A little less cynical."

"When the world is all rainbows and kitten whiskers, I'll give it a try. Until then I'm maintaining the status quo. If it ain't broke, don't fix it."

"You have a healthy ego."

"I'm self-aware. It's totally different."

"Said the man that thinks he doesn't need to change or improve. How's that workin' for you?"

"Just fine, thank you for asking." He set down his empty glass. "Tedi, would you like to dance?"

So intent on quizzing Jack, I hadn't even noticed that as couples had finished their meals they were wandering onto the makeshift dance floor on the far side of the expansive back patio.

I liked the song and it was a lovely, sunny day. I wouldn't mind a dance but I didn't want to appear to give in too easily.

"Are you asking me because you truly want to dance or are you asking me because you think it will get me to shut up and stop asking you questions?"

"It's about fifty-fifty, although you rarely stop talking. I'm getting used to it."

Jack didn't say whether he liked it or not, just that he was getting used to it.

Frankly, it was more than I could hope for with most people. I also admired the fact that he didn't lie. He just said how he felt. Few did.

"Fair enough. Let's dance."

One dance turned into several. Don't ask me how because I swear, I don't know. We were dancing and talking and the next thing I knew Amelia and Charles were cutting the cake. Everyone knew that the reception was almost over when that happened.

If you haven't learned anything about me so far, know this…I wasn't going to miss eating the cake. Not for any song, any dance, or any man. Not in this lifetime. I wasn't above throwing a few elbows in line either to get a piece with extra frosting.

"Relax, I'll get you a piece of cake."

Jack was offering to get me some cake? Really? That was…nice.

"Extra frosting, please."

I sat down at the table where Missy and Dylan were nowhere to be found. Had they exited early?

Two plates of cake appeared in front of me as Jack sat down. They both appeared to have a sufficient amount of buttercream.

"Do I get to choose which one I want?"

"You get to have both. I took two because there are two of us but there's no law that says you can't eat both. If you want to."

I did want to. Very much.

"You don't want cake?"

Please say no. Please say no.

"I like pies and ice cream better. Go ahead. I'm stuffed."

I couldn't turn down such a lovely offer. It would be rude. My mother would be upset if I was rude.

"You know me so well, Jack. Thank you."

He handed me a fork and I dug into the first piece, the sugar exploding on my tongue and sending a rush of energy all the way to my toes. Cake good. Sugar good. I'd made the primitive part of my brain ecstatic.

I was busy shoveling cake into my face but Jack apparently had something on his mind. His fingers drummed on the table and then he shifted around in his chair so he was looking at me directly.

"So I was wondering if maybe–"

Whatever he was going to say was drowned out by loud voices coming ever closer. Laura and Jessica were having a huge argument in the middle of the wedding reception. Laura was clearly trying to get away from Jessica but the younger woman was tenacious and followed closely behind. Finally, Laura rounded on Jessica, her finger pointed right at her.

"You were having an affair with my husband. Admit it."

If anyone was snoozing during this reception, they were awake now. Apparently, Laura thought that every woman was having an affair with her late husband. How did he ever have time to sleep or work?

Jessica snorted. "I wasn't interested in your lame old has-been husband. Although I will say that he tried, but I slapped him down like he deserved. He was a creep and you know it. That's why you were having an affair with Darrell. Don't bother to deny it. Everyone knew."

Laura's face was bright red and there was spittle at the corner of her mouth. She looked angry enough to kill...or at least smack Jessica. Hard.

"I was not. That's a lie."

Jessica, on the other hand, didn't look perturbed in the least. If anything, she looked smug.

"It's not a lie. Everyone on the set knew, including your dearly departed husband. He was looking to get a divorce and that would have left you with nothing because of the prenup. If anyone killed Brock Mandrell it was you. You hated him and you wanted him dead. Admit it."

Her shoulders rapidly rising and falling, Laura shook her head as a flashbulb went off. Then another. Somehow Jack had stood up and next thing I knew he was dragging a reporter out of the bushes. How long had he been lying in wait to get a story?

Looks like his patience paid off.

He held the squirming and protesting reporter by the back of his shirt. "Tedi, do you want to press charges against this man for trespassing?"

"Yes, I do," I proclaimed loudly. All the guests had stopped talking and were watching the scene unfold in front of us. "To the fullest extent of the law."

More squeaky protests from the man, but Jack wasn't having any of it. He handed the reporter off to one of his deputies who was in attendance and then turned his attention to the ladies, who suddenly seemed to realize they'd played out their drama for an audience.

"I'd like to speak to both of you ladies down at the station, please. Right away."

"I want my lawyer," Laura immediately said. "I won't say a word until he's here."

"Spoken just like a guilty person," Jessica jeered.

Jack sent her a dark look before turning back to Laura. "That is your right. Give them a call. I also want to speak to Darrell Kennedy."

Laura shrugged. "I don't know where he is."

Jack turned to the deputy who had hold of the reporter. "Take him to the station and book him. I'll find Kennedy."

The deputy dragged the reporter out of the party and Jack spoke to the two women but I couldn't hear what he was saying. Whatever it was, they both looked suitably chastened before heading back upstairs. Most of the guests had returned to whatever they were doing now that all the fun was over.

"I'll help you find Darrell Kennedy," I offered. "He should be in his room. He was saying earlier that he wasn't feeling well."

Jack shook his head. "No, you stay here. I can get him. I just have a few more questions for him based on what I heard today."

"Do you think Laura is guilty?"

"I don't know but she has a strong motive. Assuming what Jessica Hornsby said is true. That's why I need to talk to Kennedy. But even if she had a strong motive for her husband, that doesn't mean she killed Bill Warner."

"You think we could have two killers in town?"

"Stranger things have happened."

Especially in Ravenmist. Jack didn't know the half of it.

DAISY INSISTED THAT I not lift a finger to help clean up after the wedding, but after all these years hosting events I had a system which I was happy to share. Within a few hours we had most of the inn set to rights and the rest would be done later.

Kicking off my blue pumps, I closed the door to my apartment behind me and let out a long, deep sigh of relief. I was planning an evening of nothing more than vegging out in front of the television and eating another piece of wedding cake – thoughtfully provided by Daisy. I'd earned a quiet night to myself. In fact, I might take a hot bath, too. My feet were killing me.

Edward and Terrence were sitting at my kitchen table, as usual these days, leaning over the laptop and barely noticing my presence.

"Did you have fun at the wedding?" I asked, grabbing a bottle of water from the fridge. "I think Daisy did a great job putting it together."

They both looked up as if just realizing that I was there. This movie was all-consuming but they were certainly enjoying themselves. Maybe I needed a hobby like that. I used to hunt ghosts but now there was no need.

"We're looking at the footage we shot today," Terrence explained. "It's going to make a great addition to your documentary."

Edward nodded in agreement. "This is going to be groundbreaking. So many spirits don't realize that they can have an active and fulfilling afterlife. They don't have to cross over if they don't want to."

"Don't let Missy hear you say that."

"It's the truth."

"It's the truth in Ravenmist. It's not the same everywhere," I pointed out. "Other towns don't have the energy that we have."

"Then we need to find out how we got this energy and make sure that the dead everywhere have it," Edward said. "I thought you were working on finding out where it came from."

"I am but these things take time. I'm going to take a hot bath and then watch television in bed. Don't work too late, okay?"

"We won't, Tedi." Terrence promised. "We only have about another hour of footage to go through."

It would not be a good thing for every town to have its own demon. Just…no. But I'd happily give ours away to anyone that wants it.

Free to good home.

Chapter Eighteen

THE NEXT MORNING, I was moving slow after such a crazy day. Somehow, I crawled into the shower and then dressed myself presentably. Being an adult wasn't all it was cracked up to be. I had a list of things to do and a magic fairy wasn't going to fly in and wave a wand.

At least I don't think so. It could happen, though. In this town, anything was possible.

Demons might not be welcome but I'd roll out the red carpet for cleaning fairies.

Terrence was at the kitchen table again when I came out to eat breakfast. I slipped two pieces of bread into the toaster and poured myself a glass of orange juice. I'd get coffee in the dining room on the way to my office. It might be Sunday but there were a few items I needed to knock off my to-do list. Then I might call Missy and see if she wanted to drive into the next town over and do some shopping.

"I hope you haven't been looking at the computer screen all night. It's not good for your eyes."

I ignored the fact that Terrence was dead. Surely if blue light was bad for humans it wasn't good for those in-between, either.

"I rested a little. You know I don't have to sleep like you do."

He said it as if he felt sorry for me. Being alive and all.

"Did you send Edward home?"

"Hours ago. He was getting on my nerves."

Really? How interesting.

"I thought you and Edward were buddies now."

Terrence shrugged. "We are but I still think he can be annoying. He likes to boss people around."

That didn't shock me in the least.

"You don't let him tell you what to do, do you?"

"No, so sometimes he goes off to pout."

"Is that where he is now?"

"Yes, he'll come back when he's done."

I sat down at the table with my toast and juice. "I am glad that you're getting out more. This documentary has been a terrific project for you."

Terrence's face lit up, and a smile grew on his boyish face. "Do you want to see what we have so far?"

Of course, I did. I wanted to support my ghost friend in his endeavors and to be honest, I was curious as to what was in this film. They'd interviewed a heck of a lot of spirits, and I wondered what they all had to say about the in-between and sharing Ravenmist with the living.

Terrence cued up the movie at the beginning, the opening scene in Missy's bookstore where Edward lived. The documentary tried to show a sort of "day in the life" of a ghost in

Ravenmist, the opportunities and the difficulties. There was definitely an optimistic air about this film, very pro not-going-into-the light. Missy's head was going to explode when she saw it.

We were about halfway through when the film showed the outside of the theater and the quaint restaurant next door. I caught a glimpse of Sasha and then Laura. I watched closely but I didn't see Darrell Jenkins. He'd said he was outside in the square. That didn't mean he wasn't, however. It was hard to tell the timing of this footage. Before or during Brock Mandrell's murder?

"Do you have any more film footage from that day outside the theater, Terrence? Some that you've edited out?"

"Sure, I do. We've made a bunch of cuts. Otherwise this documentary would be about ten hours long."

"Can I see it? It's really important."

Had Darrell lied about his whereabouts? I was determined to find out.

AFTER WATCHING THE edited footage, I tried to find Darrell but he wasn't in his room. Tina at the front desk said she'd seen him exit the inn about an hour ago and he'd said something about getting brunch.

I headed straight for The Grateful Raven.

I know what you're thinking. You're thinking that I should

talk to Jack about this first, but how can I?

Hey Jack, a couple of ghosts are filming a documentary about life in-between and they have some footage of the theater at the time of the murder that might be evidence.

He would think I'd lost my mind.

I wasn't planning on being alone with Darrell or anything. I'd learned that when Lorna had heaved Howard the Fern at my head. We'd be in public with lots of people around and I'd be safe as a kitten. I wasn't about to take any stupid chances.

Darrell was walking out of the diner when I arrived. I waved to get his attention and he paused on the sidewalk.

"I was hoping I'd catch you," I said, catching my breath. I really needed to start working out. I was breathless from a slow jog. "There was something I needed to talk to you about."

"Anything you need. How about we chat while we walk back to the inn?"

That sounded good. There were plenty of pedestrians out and about. We wouldn't be alone by a long shot.

"Did you want to talk about that messy business with Laura and Jessica?"

Well…no. But I wouldn't say no if he wanted to discuss it.

"I assume the sheriff talked to you about it."

I knew for a fact that he had.

"He did. It's a sad business. I had to fire Jessica over it."

I hadn't seen Laura or Jessica this morning and I hadn't expected to. Jack had given them strict instructions to lay low and stay out of the newspapers until this was all cleared up.

"You fired her for lying?"

Darrell smiled and shook his head. "I fired her for talking about my private business."

"So you were having an affair with Laura."

"She's a desperately unhappy woman and Brock was an idiot husband. It wasn't serious, though. Just two people who happened to find themselves thrown together for a few months while we made the movie."

"Did Brock know?"

Darrell shrugged. "I have no idea. Maybe. He was busy sleeping with any female that crossed his path. I doubt he would have even cared, to be honest."

"Life in Hollywood sure is different."

"It's the land of dreams. Anything is possible."

This was the opening I'd been looking for.

"A few of my friends are actually making an amateur documentary. Nothing elaborate, but it's interesting to watch the process. In fact, they have some footage of the theater at the time of Brock's death."

"How can you be sure of the time?"

"The bell tower chimed eight in the footage. That was the time of death according to the coroner." I deliberately slowed my steps, wanting to watch Darrell's expression. "You said that you were outside at the time taking a call but I didn't see you anywhere."

A flicker of...something crossed Darrell's face but was gone as quickly as it had come.

"You must be mistaken. I was outside." He held up his phone. "I was making a call. It's in my call history."

"You definitely weren't there."

"Your friends probably filmed from a different angle. That's all."

I am math challenged but I passed geometry with a B. I wasn't sure about this whole angle explanation.

"You said that you stepped out of the front doors to take a call. Their film shows the front doors very clearly."

"I probably stepped around the side of the building or behind a tree. I don't really remember. Just because you can't see me doesn't mean I wasn't there."

Darrell was beginning to sound a lot like my ex-husband David who used to tell me that I was confused and if only I understood I'd agree with whatever he was saying.

But I wasn't confused, and I did understand. I just didn't agree.

"Then wouldn't I have seen you step outside the doors and then around the building? I didn't see you at all."

Darrell's hand clamped onto my arm, his fingers tightening painfully.

"If you know what's good for you, you'll stop meddling in things you don't understand."

Uh oh. I had a bad feeling about this. I'd assumed that Darrell would have a reasonable explanation but he didn't and now he was agitated. Red-faced and sweating, his grip on my arm was like a steel band. I tried to jerk my arm away but he wasn't letting go.

Thank goodness we were in public. He couldn't do anything out here in full view of everyone.

"It's okay, Darrell. It's all fine."

I tried using my best soothing tone but it had no effect whatsoever. If anything, he appeared more upset than before.

"I hated Brock Mandrell. He was going to take everything from me. Everything. He was a horrible human being and he deserved what he got."

Was this some sort of confession?

"That's true. Few people liked him."

"The world is a better place." Darrell's pace had picked up and he was practically dragging me along with him as I tried to yank my arm away. So much for being out in public. Didn't anyone notice, for heaven's sake? "I did everyone a favor. People should thank me."

Okay, that sounded like a confession to me. Now how do I get out of his clutches? Should I scream? I was pretty sure someone would come to my aid and that they wouldn't think I was playing a prank. I wasn't the greatest screamer but I think I could get someone's attention.

Abruptly stopping, Darrell stared down the road to where a truck was barreling in our direction. He didn't say anything but he had a look in his eye that I didn't like in the least. My suspicions were confirmed when he began moving toward the street and trying to take me with him. I had a terrible feeling that Darrell Jenkins was planning to throw himself – and me – in front of that big truck.

This time I found my voice, screaming so loud my lungs hurt. I dug my heels in and pulled backward with all of my strength, cursing the fact that I always talked about exercising but never actually did it. If I could just get out of this predicament, I'd turn over a new leaf. I'd be a fitness machine. I'd eat kale.

Just let me get out of this alive.

I was trying to bend his fingers back when another hand came down on Darrell's, breaking his grip on me so I crumpled to the ground with an indignant bump. The truck drove by harmlessly and I took a moment to begin breathing again before looking up at my rescuer's face. They deserved effusive thanks from me. Possibly flowers and fine chocolates. Whatever they wanted, I'd try and get for them.

It was Jack, of course.

He'd slapped cuffs on Darrell and was reading him his rights. And he was scowling. As usual. Some things never change. Even in Ravenmist. Thank goodness.

I could repay Jack with pie and ice cream.

Can you make kale into ice cream? Asking for a friend.

Chapter Nineteen

THE TOWN WAS back to normal again. The movie stars were gone and the reporters with them. Once again, the press in Ravenmist consisted solely of Gus and after all that had happened, he had decided to take a vacation and go fishing. No local newspaper for awhile.

I'd spoken to my friend Sasha and given her the news. She'd told me that she had landed a pivotal role in a new blockbuster and I was thrilled for her. She deserved it. Cara had flown to Los Angeles the day before to start work on her cop series that would debut in the fall. She was still singing Jack's praises and telling everyone how much he'd helped her.

Jessica Hornsby had run off with an Argentinian polo player and got married in Las Vegas. Pictures of the wedding were blasted all over and she looked really happy. Laura Mandrell had announced her return to the silver screen with the lead in a romantic comedy and she had also set up a scholarship fund in her late husband's name for students who wanted to pursue the arts. When she'd left town – right before she climbed in her limo – she'd told me that while Ravenmist was perfectly lovely she was never coming back again.

I didn't blame her.

Darrell Jenkins was charged with the murders of Brock Mandrell and Bill Warner and held without bail in the county jail. He'd assembled a fantasy team of attorneys to defend him and they were in the news almost every day talking about this ruling or that filing. They were constantly beating the "reasonable doubt" drum and it might work. Strangers things had happened. In all likelihood, the trial was months away. The prosecution was leaning on the fingerprint evidence on the murder weapon.

That's right. My mother's clumsiness had finally paid off. The lab had matched the ballistics from the gun we'd found in the theater to the bullets in both Brock Mandrell and Bill Warner. They'd also pulled a thumbprint from Darrell Jenkins. That's why Jack had been Johnny-on-the-spot the day Darrell tried to throw both of us in front of a truck. He'd been looking for the director to arrest him.

Darrell's lawyers were questioning the veracity of the fingerprint evidence and the lab's procedures. The incarcerated director had given an interview a few days ago, saying that he might have touched the gun when Laura showed it to him.

Yep, he was still beating the *Laura did it* drum. And downplaying his own motives.

When Jack had arrested that reporter for trespassing, the guy had spilled his guts about everything he knew about Darrell, Warner, and Mandrell. Turns out he knew quite a lot. Brock knew that Darrell was having an affair with his wife so he – with the help of Bill Warner who had connections at the studio – had convinced the bigwigs to jettison the director for the sequels. They were also smearing Darrell's name all over Hollywood, making it impossible to get another directing gig. According to the reporter, Darrell wanted revenge.

Jack always talks about the big three motives: money, love, or revenge. This one had an element of each.

Edward and Terrence were the real heroes, of course, but no one could know that. They were still working on their documentary and talking about eventually releasing it on the internet so that the entire world would know about ghosts and the in-between. Edward said he wanted to be on the cover of *People* magazine. The whole idea still gives me frequent headaches. It's like a huge boulder rolling down a hill and picking up speed. I needed to stop it before it flattens everyone at the bottom but there's no good way to do that without getting creamed myself.

We still had the issue of the demon. That hadn't suddenly disappeared, unfortunately, and it was the main topic of conversation whenever Missy and I were together. Today was no exception.

"I think we need pie," I said, pushing my almost empty plate away. We were having lunch at Daisy's and I'd demolished a cheeseburger but had saved room for dessert by only eating half of my fries. Thinking ahead. "Coconut or lemon."

"I want the chocolate," Missy stated, her lips pursed in thought. "Or maybe the cherry. I can't decide."

"So you're going to talk to your uncle tonight?"

"I am. He's finally back from spring vacation. I'm hoping he can use his connections and help us find a way to reveal the identity of the demon. Grandma is working on it, too. She's up in Peoria with my cousins going through every book in their house hoping to find an answer to our problem."

The waitress cleared our plates and took our pie order. Coconut and chocolate.

"What if…we can't find anything?"

I'd been thinking about that scenario more and more and losing too much sleep.

Our dessert was slid in front of us and we both dug in, stress making us eat too many sweets. At least it did for me. I didn't know Missy's story.

We ate quietly until it was all gone, our stomachs full and our minds buzzing with activity.

"If we can't solve this, we have to have faith in the good demon," Missy finally said, breaking the silence. "The war between good and evil has been going on since the dawn of time. So far good seems to be winning so the demon might not even need our help. He or she might have this all under control."

"I want to believe that."

But I was a control freak who didn't like the thought of humanity depending on some unknown entity to save it.

It wasn't easy being an optimist under these conditions.

I also wasn't sure as Missy that good was winning these wars. There were days that evil seemed to have the upper hand. Then

I'd see a puppy and it was all good again.

Cynics can like puppies. And cotton candy. And sunshine. I do think unicorns are ridiculous, though.

The bell over the door rang and Jack walked in, his gaze running over the room and then resting on me. I hadn't had much time to talk to him lately but I'd seen him regularly in my kitchen.

Eating.

But I was fine with it. I did owe him my life.

Missy waved him over. "Hey, Sheriff. Here for lunch?"

He checked his watch and nodded. "I've got a few minutes so I thought I'd stop in for a quick bite. How are you ladies today?"

"We're fine," Missy assured him. "Take my seat. I have to be getting back to the bookshop anyway. Tedi, call me later about the movie."

Missy and I were going to see the new romantic comedy at the theater. Bill Warner and Samuel had given it two thumbs up.

Jack took Missy's side of the booth and the waitress bustled over to take his order. Everyone knew that Jack didn't have much patience.

"Is Tyler ready for the end of school? There's not much left of the year."

"Three weeks," Jack replied, sipping his coffee. "I've been trying to convince him to settle down and start studying for finals but he's going to put it off until the last minute like he does everything else."

"I once learned an entire semester of art history in one night."

"Because it was art history, Tedi. How hard could it be? And please don't tell Tyler that. He doesn't need any encouragement to be a procrastinator. He comes by it naturally."

"Is his mother a procrastinator?"

Now why did I ask that? Sometimes I just want to slap myself.

"Yes, she is."

Change the subject. Quick.

"So have you heard anything about Darrell Jenkins' case?"

"He's going to go down fighting. He's already talking about the book and movie rights to his story. Personally, I think he's guilty but proving it is the prosecutor's job. I handed over all the evidence so I'm out of it."

"Will you have to testify at the trial?"

I always knew when Jack was scheduled to do that because he wore a suit that day.

Rubbing his chin, he cleared his throat. "Yes, and you probably will too, Tedi. He's charged with your attempted murder. Plus, he confessed to you and only you."

"Right before he was going to throw us under the large tires of a truck. I remember it quite clearly."

"I've been meaning to ask you...what made him do that? What were you talking about that he suddenly confessed?"

I'd never told Jack about the film footage because I couldn't explain it. My hope was that the prosecution wouldn't need it but I wasn't above sending it to them anonymously.

I shrugged as if I didn't have a clue. "I mentioned Laura and Brock, that's all. He was under a lot of stress and he must have cracked at that particular moment. That's my only explanation."

Jack gave me a shrewd look but he didn't challenge my account of that day.

"Murderers don't always do things that make sense, especially when they're under stress and think that the police are closing in. But it's all over and now this town can get back to normal. Unless you have any festivals or parties planned. I think you need to start giving me a head's up on those."

Haha. Jack's a comedian.

"Nothing until the Fall Festival. Just the usual summer guests. How about you, Jack? What do you have planned this summer?"

"Not much." Jack's meal – a turkey sandwich and fries – was placed in front of him. "Tyler is going to spend most of the summer with his mom, of course."

"So you'll be footloose and fancy free. Nice."

There wasn't anything about Jack Garrett that was footloose. Or fancy. Or free.

"I'll have some time on my hands." He picked up a fry but didn't pop it into his mouth. "I was thinking that you and I might have dinner one night. What do you think?"

Uh...what? What did he say? Did Jack just...ask me out on a date?

"Dinner?"

I sounded like a parrot. A really dumb one.

"Dinner. You and me. What do you say?"

What did I say? I was going to say no, of course. I wasn't looking for a man or romance or complications in my life. I liked things just as they were. I wasn't even sure that I liked Jack all that much. This friend stuff was difficult enough. No, absolutely no.

"Yes, that would be nice."

I am an optimist.

Thank you for reading Ghosts, Lies, and Videotape.
Tedi and Jack will be back soon with a new whodunit! Keep
up with all of the new releases in the series by visiting
www.oliviajaymes.com

About The Author

Olivia Jaymes is a wife, mother, lover of sexy romance and cozy mysteries, and caffeine addict. She lives with her husband, son, and two spoiled dogs in central Florida and spends her days typing on her computer with a canine on her lap.

She is currently working on a new cozy mystery series – *A Ravenmist Whodunnit* – in addition to her other ongoing romance series.

Visit Olivia Jaymes at

www.OliviaJaymes.com